H. Irving Hancock

Uncle Sam's Boys With Pershing's Troops

H. Irving Hancock

Uncle Sam's Boys With Pershing's Troops

1st Edition | ISBN: 978-3-75236-118-6

Place of Publication: Frankfurt am Main, Germany

Year of Publication: 2020

Outlook Verlag GmbH, Germany.

UNCLE SAM'S BOYS WITH PERSHING'S TROOPS

By H. Irving Hancock

CHAPTER I

His jaw set firmly, his keen, fiery eyes roving over the group before him, the gray-haired colonel of infantry closed his remarks with these words:

"Gentlemen, the task set for the officers of the United States Army is to produce, with the least possible delay, the finest fighting army in the world. Our own personal task is to make this, the Ninety-ninth, the finest regiment of infantry in that army.

"You have heard, at some length, what is expected of you. Any officer present, of any grade, who does not feel equal to the requirements I have laid down will do well to seek a transfer to some other regiment or branch of the service, or to send in his resignation as a military officer."

Rising to their feet behind the long, uncovered pine board mess tables at which they had sat listening and taking notes, the eyes of the colonel's subordinate officers glistened with enthusiasm. Instead of showing any trace of dissent they greeted their commanding officer's words with a low murmur of approval that grew into a noisy demonstration, then turned into three rousing cheers.

"And a tiger!" shouted a young lieutenant, in a bull-like voice that was heard over the racket.

Colonel Cleaves, though he did not unbend much before the tumult, permitted a gleam of satisfaction to show itself in his fine, rugged features.

"Good!" he said quietly, in a firm voice. "I feel assured that we shall all pull together for the common weal and for the abiding glory of American arms."

Gathering up the papers that he had, during his speech, laid out on the table before him, the colonel stepped briskly down the central aisle of the mess-room. As it was a confidential meeting of regimental officers, and no enlisted man was present, one of the second lieutenants succeeded in being first to reach the door. Throwing it open, he came smartly to attention, saluting as the commanding officer passed through the doorway. Then the door closed.

"Good!" cried Captain Dick Prescott. "That was straight talk all the way through."

"Hit the mark or leave the regiment!" voiced Captain Greg Holmes enthusiastically.

"Be a one hundred per cent. officer, or get out of the service!" agreed another comrade.

The tumult had already died down. The officers, from Lieutenant-Colonel Graves down to the newest "shave-tail" or second lieutenant, acted as by common impulse when they pivoted slowly about on their heels, glancing at each other with earnest smiles.

"Gentlemen, our job has been cut out for us. We know the price of success, and we know what failure would mean for us, personally or collectively. Going over to quarters, Sands?"

Thrusting a hand through the arm of Major Sands, Lieutenant-Colonel Graves started down the aisle. Little groups followed, and the mess-room of that company barracks was speedily emptied.

Hard work, not age, had brought the gray frosting into the hair of Colonel Cleaves; he was forty-seven years old, and not many months before he had been only a major.

The time was early in September, in the year 1917. War had been declared against Germany on April 6th. In the middle of July the Ninety-o-ninth Infantry had been called into existence. Regiments were then being added to the Regular Army. Two or three hundred trained soldiers and several hundred recruits had made up the beginnings of the regiment. Prescott and Holmes had been among the latest of the captains sent to the regiment, arriving in August. And now Colonel Cleaves had just joined his command on orders from Washington.

With forty men in the headquarters company and some fifty in the machine-gun company, the rifle companies on this September day averaged about seventy men. Nor had a full complement of officers yet arrived.

Dick Prescott and Greg Holmes, lately first lieutenants, as readers of former volumes of this series are aware, had received their commissions as captains just before joining the Ninety-ninth.

"This regiment is scheduled to go over at an early date," Colonel Cleaves had informed his regimental officers, at the conference of which we have just witnessed the close. "Headquarters and machine-gun companies must be raised to their respective quotas of men, and each rifle company must be increased from seventy to two hundred and fifty men each. New recruits will arrive every week. These men must be whipped into shape. Gentlemen, I expect your tireless aid in making this the finest infantry regiment in the American line."

One or two glances at Colonel Cleaves, when he was talking earnestly, were enough to show the observer that this officer meant all he said. Shirkers, among either officers or men, would receive scant consideration in his regiment.

Camp Berry, at which the Ninety-ninth and the Hundredth were stationed, lay in one of the prettiest parts of Georgia. Needless to say the day was one of sweltering heat and the regimental officers, as they filed out of the company barracks that had been used for holding the conference, fanned themselves busily with their campaign hats. Each, however, as he struck the steps leading to the ground, placed his campaign hat squarely on his head.

"Some pace the K.O. has set for us," murmured Greg, as he and Dick started to walk down the company street.

"And we must keep that pace if we hope to last in Colonel Cleaves's regiment," Dick declared, with conviction. "Time was when an officer in the Regular Army could look forward to remaining an officer as long as he was physically fit and did not disgrace himself. But in this war any officer, regular or otherwise, will find himself laid on the shelf whenever he fails to produce his full share of usefulness."

"Do you think it's really as bad as that, Prescott?" demanded Captain Cartwright, who was walking just behind them.

"Worse!" Dick replied dryly and briefly.

Cartwright sighed, then took a tighter grip on the swagger stick that he carried jauntily in his right hand. Cartwright was a smart, soldierly looking chap, but was well known as an officer who was not addicted to hard work.

Past three or four barrack buildings on the street the chums walked, Cartwright still keeping just behind them.

"Look at the work of Sergeant Mock, will you?" demanded Greg, halting short as they came to the edge of one of the drill grounds.

Mock belonged to Greg's own company. At this moment the sergeant was busy, or should have been, drilling what was supposed to be a platoon, though to-day it consisted of only two corporals' squads, or sixteen men in all.

Greg Holmes's eyes opened wide with disgust as he watched the drilling, unseen by the sergeant.

The platoon had just wheeled and marched off by fours. The cadence was too slow, the men looked slouchy and showed no signs whatever of spirit.

"Perhaps the sergeant isn't feeling well," remarked Dick, with a smile.

"He won't be feeling well after he has talked with me," Greg uttered between his teeth.

To the further limit of the drill ground the sergeant marched his platoon, then wheeled them and brought them back again. As he came about the sergeant caught sight of his company commander. In an undertone he gave an order that brought his men along at greater speed than they had gone.

"Halt!" ordered the sergeant, and brought up his hand in salute to the officers.

"Sergeant Mock," called Holmes, in a low, even voice, "turn the men over to a corporal and come here."

Hastily, and flushing, Sergeant Mock came forward.

"How are the men feeling?" Greg inquired, after signaling the corporal now in charge to continue the drilling.

"Tired, sir," replied Mock, with a shamefaced look.

"And how is the sergeant feeling?" Greg went on, as the corporal led the men across the drill ground, this time at a sharper pace and correcting any fault in soldierly bearing that he observed.

"All right, sir," replied the sergeant.

"Then, if you're feeling all right, Sergeant Mock," Greg continued in as even a voice as before, "explain to me why you were marching the platoon at a cadence of about ninety, instead of the regulation hundred and twenty steps per minute. Tell me why the alignment of the fours was poor, and why the men were allowed to march without paying the slightest heed to their bearing."

Though there was nothing at all sharp in the company commander's voice, Mock knew that he was being "called," and, in fact, was perilously close to being "cussed out."

"The——the day is hot, sir, and——and I knew the men were about played out," stammered Mock.

"How long have you been in the Army, sergeant?" Greg continued.

"About two years and a half, sir."

"In all that time did you ever know officers or enlisted men to be excused from full performance of ordered duty on account of the weather?"

"N-n-no, sir."

"Then why did you start a new system on your own authority?" Greg asked quietly.

Mock tried to answer, opened his mouth, in fact, and uttered a few incoherent sounds, which quickly died in his throat.

"Sergeant Mock," said Greg, "we have just heard from our commanding officer. He demands the utmost from every officer, non-com and private. Are you prepared, and resolved, from this moment, to give the utmost that is in you at all times?"

"Yes, sir!" replied Mock with greatemphasis.

"You mean what you are saying, Sergeant?"

"Yes, sir."

"Very good, then," continued the young captain. "I am going to take your word for it this time. But if I ever find you slacking or shirking again, I am going to go to the colonel immediately and ask him to 'break' you back to the ranks."

"Yes, sir," assented Mock, saluting.

"Are you fully familiar with all your drill work?"

"Yes, sir."

"Then remember that our enemies, the German soldiers, are men who are drilled and drilled until they are perfect in their work, and that their discipline is amazing. Keep the fact in mind that we can hardly hope to whip our enemies unless we are at least as good soldiers as they. That is all. Go back to your men, Sergeant."

Standing stiffly erect, Sergeant Mock brought up his right hand in a crisp salute, then wheeled and walked briskly back to join his men. Greg turned as if to say that he did not feel the need of remaining to watch the rebuked sergeant.

"By Jove!" uttered Captain Cartwright. "I do wish, Holmes, you'd come over and dress down some of my non-coms. I've been trying for three days to put 'pep' into some of them, and the K.O. frowned at me this morning."

"Non-com" is the Army abbreviation for "non-commissioned officers"—corporals and sergeants—while "K.O." is Army slang for commanding officer.

Arrived at an unpainted wooden barracks, in size and appearance just like those of the enlisted men, the three captains entered and walked up a flight of stairs to the floor above. Here they passed through a narrow corridor with doors on both sides that bore the cards of the officers who slept behind the respective doors. Cartwright went to his own room, while Greg followed Dick into the latter's quarters.

Plain enough was the room, seven and a half feet wide and ten feet in length, with a single sliding window at the front. Walls and ceiling, like the floor, were of pine boards. There were shelves around two sides of the room, with clothing hooks underneath. Under the window was a desk, with a cot to one side; the rest of the furniture consisted of two folding camp chairs.

Entering, Dick hung up his campaign hat on one of the hooks, Greg doing the same. On account of the heat of the day neither young captain wore a tunic. Each unbuttoned the top button of his olive drab Army shirt before he dropped into a chair.

"What do you think of the new K.O.?" Dick asked, as he picked a newspaper up from the desk and started to fan himself.

"He means business," Greg returned. "I am glad he does," Dick went on. "This is no time for slack soldiering. Greg, I'll feel consoled for working eighteen hours a day if it results in making the Ninety-ninth the best infantry regiment of the line."

"Can it be done?" Greg inquired.

"Yes."

"But I've a hunch that every other regiment is striving for the same honor," Captain Holmes continued. "Ours isn't the only K.O. who covets the honor of commanding the best regiment of 'em all."

"It can be done," Dick insisted, "and I say it must be done."

"Yet other regiments would be so close to us in excellence that it would be hard to name the one that is really best."

"In that case we wouldn't have won the honor," Dick smilingly insisted.

"Then consider that fellow Cartwright," Greg added, lowering his voice a bit. "He's a born shirker, and one weak company would make a regiment that much poorer."

"If Cartwright shirks, then mark my word that he'll be dropped," Dick rejoined quickly. "But Greg, man, this is war-time, and the biggest and most serious war in which we were ever engaged. There must be no doubts——no ifs or buts. We must have a regiment one hundred per cent. perfect. I'm going to do my share with a company one hundred percent. good, even if I don't find time for any sleep."

Up the corridor there sounded a knock at a door. Something was said in a low voice. Then the knock was repeated on Prescott's door.

"Come in!" called Dick.

An orderly entered saluting.

"Orders from the adjutant, sir," said the soldier, handing Prescott a folded paper. He handed one like it to Greg, then saluted and left the room, knocking at the next door.

"Company drill from one to two-thirty," summarized Prescott, glancing through the typewritten words on the unfolded sheet. "Practice march by battalions from two-forty-five to three-forty-five. Squad drill from four o'clock until retreat. That looks brisk, Greg."

"Doesn't it?" asked Holmes, without too plain signs of enthusiasm. "Company drill and the hike call for our presence, preferably, and yet I've paper work enough to keep me busy until evening mess."

"Paper work," so-called, is the bane of life for the company commander. It consists of keeping, making and signing records, of the keeping and inspection of accounts; it deals with requisitions for supplies and an endless number of reports.

"I have a barrelful of paper work, too," Dick admitted. "But I'm going to see everything going well on the drill ground before I go near company office."

"All good things must end," grunted Greg, rising to his feet, "even this rest. Mess will be on in eight minutes."

The instant that the door had closed Dick drew off his olive drab shirt, drew out a lidded box from under the bed and deposited the shirt therein, next restoring the box to place bring out a basin from under the bed and placing it on a chair, he found towel and soap and busied himself with washing up. His toilet completed, he took a clean shirt from a bundle on one of the neatly arranged shelves and donned the garment. A few more touches, and, spick-and-span, clean and very soldierly looking, he descended to the ground floor. A glance into the mess-room showed him that the noon meal was not yet ready, so be sauntered to the doorway, remaining just inside out of the sun's rays.

Other officers gathered quickly. A waiter from mess appeared at the inner doorway, speaking a quiet word that caused the regiment's officers, except the colonel and his staff, to file inside.

Plain pine tables, without cloths, long pine benches nailed to the floor— officers' mess was exactly like that of the enlisted men, save that officers' mess was provided with heavy crockery, while in the company mess-rooms the men ate from aluminum mess-kits.

Most of the food was already in place on the table. The meal began with a lively hum of conversation. Occasionally some merry officer called out jokingly to some officer at another table; there was no special effort at dignified silence.

"The K.O. has our number!" exclaimed an irrepressible lieutenant.

"How so?" demanded Noll Terry, Prescott's first lieutenant.

"He knows us for a bunch of shirkers, and so he gave us the 'pep' talk this morning."

"Is the 'pep' going to work with you?" asked Noll laughingly.

"Surely! I wouldn't dare be slow, even in drawing my breath, after hearing the K.O. talk in that fashion."

"Same here," Noll nodded.

"I've been working sixteen hours a day ever since I hit camp," chimed in another lieutenant. "What's the new system going to be? Eighteen hours a day?"

"Twenty, perhaps," said Greg's first lieutenant cheerfully.

The meal had been under way for fifteen minutes when Captain Cartwright entered leisurely.

"I suppose you fellows have eaten all the best stuff," he called, as he looked about and found a vacant seat, though he paused as if in no great haste to occupy it.

"Same old Cartwright," observed Greg, in an undertone to Dick. "He's late, even at mess formation."

But Cartwright heard, and wheeled about, looking half-angrily at young Captain Holmes.

"Say, Holmes, you're as free as ever with your tongue."

"Yes," Greg answered unconcernedly. "Using it to taste my food, and I've been finding the taste uncommonly pleasant."

"You use your tongue in more ways than that," snapped Captain Cartwright. "I happened to hear what you said about me in Prescott's room a few minutes ago."

"Eavesdropping?" queried Greg calmly.

"What's that?" snapped Cartwright, and his flush deepened. "See here, Holmes, I don't want any trouble with you."

9

"That shows a lively sense of discretion," smiled Greg, turning to face the other.

"But I want you to stop picking on me. Talk about somebody else for a change!"

"With pleasure," nodded Greg, as he shrugged his shoulders and turned to drop a spoonful of sugar in his second cup of coffee. "There are lots of agreeable subjects for conversation in Camp Berry."

"Meaning—?" demanded Cartwright, still standing, and scowling, for, out of the corners of his eyes, he saw that several of his brother officers were smiling.

"Meaning almost anything that you wish," continued Captain Holmes, serenely, as he stirred his coffee.

"Sit down, Cartwright," urged a low voice. "This is a gentleman's outfit," declared another voice, perhaps not intended to reach Cartwright's ears. But he heard the words and his mounting rage caused him to take a step nearer to Greg, at the same time clenching his fists.

Greg, though he realized what was taking place, did not bother to turn, but coolly raised his cup to his lips.

"Sit down," called another voice. "You're rocking the boat."

But Cartwright took a second step. It is impossible to say what would have happened, but Dick Prescott, half turning in his seat, caught the angry captain's nearer wrist in a grip of steel and fairly swang Cartwright into a vacant seat at his left. Greg was sitting at his right.

"Don't be foolish, Cartwright, and don't let the day's heat go to your head," Prescott advised. "Don't do anything you'd regret."

Though Captain Cartwright's blood was boiling there was a sense of quiet mastery in Prescott's manner and voice, combined with a quality of leadership that restrained the angry man for the next few seconds, during which Dick turned to a waiter to say:

"This meat is cold. Bring some hot meat for Captain Cartwright, and more vegetables. Try some of this salad, Cartwright—it's good."

Instantly the officers, looking eagerly on, turned their glances away and began general conversation again, for they were quick to see that Dick's usual tact was at least postponing a quarrel.

"It will be a hot afternoon for drill, won't it?" Dick asked, in the next breath, and in a low tone.

"Maybe," grunted Cartwright. "But perhaps I shall find still hotter work before the drill-call sounds."

"Nonsense!" said Dick quickly. "After the K.O.'s talk this morning, don't start anything that will take our mind off our work."

"I've got to have a bit more than an explanation from Holmes," the sulky captain continued, though in a low voice.

"Cartwright," said Dick, in an authoritative undertone, "I don't want you to start anything in that direction until you've had a good talk with me!"

There the matter ended for the moment. Dick joined in the general conversation. Presently Cartwright tried to, but the officers to whom he addressed his remarks replied either so briefly or so coolly that the captain realized that he was not popular at the present time.

"Holmes will make trouble for any one who doesn't toady to him," thought Captain Cartwright moodily. "I can see that I've got to make it my business to take the conceit and arrogance out of him."

At almost the same moment, over in a company barracks, Sergeant Mock, as he chewed his food gloomily, was reflecting:

"So Captain Holmes will call me down before a lot of officers, will he? He'll order me to show more 'pep,' will he, the slave-driver? And if I don't he'll break me, eh?"

"Breaking" a non-commissioned officer is securing his reduction to the grade of private.

"The captain is so lazy himself that he doesn't know a good man when he sees one," Mock told himself angrily.

Then he added, threateningly to himself:

"He'd better not try it. If he does, he'll sure wish he hadn't. Since this war began even the officers are only on probation, and I've brains enough to find a way to put him in bad with the regimental K.O."

"What's the matter, Mock, don't you like your food?" asked the sergeant seated at his left. "You're scowling something fierce."

"It isn't the chow," Sergeant Mock retorted gruffly.

"Must be the heat, then—-or a call-down," observed his brother sergeant.

"Never you mind!" retorted Mock. "And I'm not talking muchnow;

I want to think."

"Must have been a real 'cussing-out' that you got," grinned the other sergeant unconcernedly.

Bending over a passing soldier murmured to Mock:

"Top wants to see you in the company office when you're through eating."

The first sergeant of a company is also known, in Army parlance, as the "top sergeant" or the "top cutter."

Though he dawdled with his meal Mock did not eat much more. Finally he rose, stalking sulkily from the mess-room and across the central corridor. Thrusting out a hand he turned the knob of the door of the company office and almost flung the door open, stepping haughtily inside.

"Mock," said First Sergeant Lund, looking up, "you're too old in the service to enter in that fashion. You know, as well as I do, that there is a 'knock' sign painted on the door, and that only an officer is privileged to enter without knocking. Suppose the captain had been in here when you flung in in that fashion?"

"He's no better than any one else!" retorted Mock.

Facing about in his chair Sergeant Lund briefly rested one hand on his desk, then sprang to his feet.

"Attention!" he commanded sharply.

Mock obeyed, throwing his head up, his chest out and squaring his shoulders as he dropped his hands straight along either trousers seam, though he sneered:

"Putting on officer's airs, are you, Lund?"

"No; I appear to be talking to a rookie (recruit) who happens to be wearing a sergeant chevrons," retorted the top sternly. "Sergeant Mock, in this office, or anywhere in my presence, you will refrain from making disrespectful remarks about your officers And I'd advise you to adopt that as your standard at all times and in all places. Do you get that?"

"I hear you," Mock rejoined, standing at ease again. "You wanted to see me?"

"Yes. Shortly before recall sounded I looked out of the window and noticed that you were handling the second platoon in anything but a soldierly manner. I was about to come out and speak to you when I observed the captain call you to him. He corrected your method of handling the platoon, didn't he?"

"He thought he did," Sergeant Mock responded, his lips quivering "But the tone he took, or rather the words he said to me, aren't the kind that make better soldiers of non-coms."

"So?" demanded Sergeant Lund, looking sharply into his subordinate's eyes.

"No!" Mock snapped sullenly. "When an officer wants me to do my best be's got to treat me like the gentleman that he's supposed to be."

For twenty seconds Sergeant Lund continued his staring at Mock. Then he rested a hand heavily on the other's shoulder as he said:

"Sergeant Mock, this is a man's army, training to do a nation's share in the biggest war in history. None but a man can do a man's work, and nothing but an army of real men can do the nation's work. If you fit yourself into your place, work hard enough and forget all about yourself except your oath to serve the Flag and obey your officers, I believe that you can do a real man's work. If you do anything different from that I'll knock your block off without a second word on the subject."

A hotly angry reply leaped to Sergeant Mock's lips, but he was wise enough to choke it back. For Sergeant Lund, a real man, a real soldier and a loyal American, stood before him regarding him with a look in which there was no faltering nor any doubt as to his intentions.

"That's all, Sergeant Mock," said the top, an instant later. "I'm going to keep an eye on you, and I want to be able to say a word of praise to you this evening."

"Two of a kind—-the top and the company commander," Mock growled under his breath as he went up the stairs to a squad room above.

CHAPTER II

A full minute before the bugler sounded the call Captain Dick Prescott was on hand, standing in the shadow of the end of the barracks of his company. Among other reasons he was there to note the alacrity with which his men came out of the building.

Before the notes of the call had died away most of the men of his company were on hand, his lieutenants among the first. Within saving time all the rest had appeared, except those who had been excused for one reason or another.

"A company fall in!" directed First Sergeant Kelly promptly.

As the men fell in in double rank there were a few cases of confusion, for some of the men were rookies who had joined only recently.

"Sergeant Kelly, instruct the other sergeants to see to it that each man knows his exact place in company formation," Dick ordered.

"Yes, sir," replied Kelly.

The corporals reported briskly the absentees, if any, in their squads. The counting of fours sounded next after inspection of arms.

"A little more snap in answering when fours are counted," Dick called, loudly enough for all the company to hear. "Let every man call his own number instantly and clearly. For instance, when one man has called 'two' let the man at his left call 'three' without a second's delay. In the way of good soldiering this is more important than most of you new men realize. Lieutenant Terry!"

"Sir," the first lieutenant responded, stepping forward, saluting.

"Take the company. Drill in dressings, facings, the manual of arms, wheeling and marching by twos and fours."

Then, stepping to one side, Prescott let his gaze rove over the company, from one file or rank to another. Everything that was done badly he noted. Presently, when the men were standing at ease he related his observations to Lieutenant Noll Terry, who thereupon gave the company further instruction.

Finally, when the company started across the drill ground in column of fours, Dick walked briskly into the barracks building, going to the company office, whither Sergeant Kelly had preceded him. Kelly, and a corporal and private who were there on clerical duty, rose and stood at attention as the captain entered.

"Rest," Dick commanded briefly, whereupon the corporal and the private returned to the desk at which they were working, while Dick crossed to the sergeant's desk. Seating himself there he gave close attention to the papers that Sergeant Kelly handed him. Such as required signature Captain Prescott signed. Then, for fifteen minutes, he busied himself with requisitions for clothing and equipment. After that other papers required close attention. Following that several matters of company administration had to be taken up. Finally, Sergeant Kelly handed Dick a list on which names had been written.

"These seven men have applied for pass from retreat this afternoon until reveille tomorrow morning," reported Dick's top. "I have approved them, subject to your action."

Reading quickly through the names, Prescott replied:

"Give six of them pass, but refuse it to Private Hartley. This forenoon I observed that he saluted officers very indifferently when passing them, and once Hartley had to be spoken to by an officer whom he did not see in time to salute him. In whose squad is Hartley?"

"In Corporal Aspen's, sir."

"Then direct Corporal Aspen to take Hartley aside, at any time suited to the corporal's convenience this evening. Have the corporal drill Private Hartley at least twenty minutes in saluting, with, of course, proper intervals for arm rest."

"Yes, sir. May I offer the captain a suggestion?"

"Yes."

"Aspen will be corporal in charge of quarters to-night. Hartley is sometimes a very slovenly soldier," Kelly reported. "May I direct Corporal Aspen to keep Hartley up and give the instruction in saluting after midnight? Corporal Aspen could take the man into the mess-room where none of the men would be disturbed."

"That sounds like a good idea," Dick nodded, smiling slightly. "If he has to lose some of his sleep for instruction Hartley may remember better. A soldier who offers his salutes in a slovenly fashion is always a long way from being a really good soldier. And, Sergeant, tell all the corporals that each will be held responsible for drill and instruction of their squads in the art of snappy saluting."

Glancing at his wrist watch Prescott now noted that it was within five minutes of time for the battalion practice march. Accordingly he stepped outside. His lieutenants being already on the drill ground he gave them brief directions as to the instruction to be imparted on the hike and the deficiencies in the men's work that were to be watched for. While he was still speaking the bugler sounded assembly.

Two or three minutes later the first battalion, under Major Wells, marched off the drill ground in column of fours.

As A company moved off at the head of the battalion some of the non-coms called quietly:

"Hip! hip! hip!"

At each "hip" the men stepped forward on the left foot. A few of the recruits still found difficulty in keeping step.

"Let that third four close up!" ordered Lieutenant Terry briskly. "Pay more heed to keeping the interval correctly."

When the third four closed up those behind closed in accordance, sergeants and corporals giving this matter close attention.

As it was a practice march the men continued to move in step. Company streets were left behind and the battalion moved on across a field, where later a trench system was to be installed, out past where the rifle ranges were already being constructed, and then up the gradual ascent of a low hill from which a spread-out view of the camp was to be had. On all the out-lying roads, at this time, bodies of troops were to be seen marching in various directions. At a distance these columns of men, clad in olive drab, made one think of brown caterpillars moving slothfully along. That was a distance effect, however, for the marching men did not move slowly, but kept on at the regular cadence of a hundred and twenty steps to the minute.

In less than ten minutes after the start, with the rays of the sun pouring down mercilessly on them, the soldiers began to perspire freely. Another five minutes and it was necessary to brush the perspiration out of their eyes.

Assuredly the officers felt the heat as much. Yet from time to time Captain Prescott fell out from his place at the head of the company and allowed the line to march by, observing every good, indifferent or bad feature of their marching, and correcting what he could by low spoken commands. Whenever the last of the company had passed Prescott ran along by the marching men until he had gained the head. If the men suffered acute discomfort in marching Prescott experienced more suffering in running under that hot sun. But he was intent only on the idea of having the best company in what he fondly hoped would turn out to be the best regiment in the Army.

For some minutes Greg had been aware that Sergeant Mock, of his company, was hobbling along. Now, as he turned to glance backward, he saw Mock step out of the ranks, go to the side of the road and sit down.

A glance at his wrist watch, and Greg saw that the first half-hour was nearly up. In a minute or two more, he knew Major Bell would give the order for a counter-march, and the first battalion would swing and come back on its own trail. So Captain Holmes turned and ran back to his non-commissioned officer.

"What's the matter, Sergeant?" the young captain inquired pleasantly.

Mock made as though trying to rise from the ground to stand at attention, but his lips twisted as though he were in pain.

"Rest," ordered Greg, "and tell me what ails you."

"My feet are killing me, sir," groaned the sergeant.

"That's odd," Captain Holmes commented. "You were all right at assembly —lively enough then. Has half an hour of marching used up a sound, healthy man?"

Instantly the sergeant's look became surly.

"All I know, sir, is that I could hardly stand on my feet. So I had to drop out. If you'll permit it, sir, I shall have to get back to camp the best way I can."

"If you're that badly off I'll have an ambulance sent for you," Greg went on. "But I don't understand your feet giving out so suddenly. Take off one of your shoes and the sock."

"That may not show much, but I'm suffering just the same, sir," rejoined the non-com in a grumbling tone.

"Let me see," Greg insisted.

While the sergeant was busy removing a legging and unlacing a shoe Captain Holmes glanced up the road to discover that the battalion was counter-marching.

"Be quick about it, Sergeant," Greg urged.

Moving no faster than he had to, Mock took off his shoe, then slowly turned the sock down, peeling it off.

"Is that the worst foot?" Greg demanded, in astonishment.

"I don't know, sir; they both hurt me."

"Do you want to show me the other foot, or do you wish to get back among the file closers?"

"I——I can't walk, sir."

Down on one knee went Greg, carefully inspecting the foot and feeling it. The skin was clean, rosy, firm.

"Why there isn't a sign of a blister," Captain Holmes declared. "Nor is there an abrasion of any kind, or any callous. There isn't even a corn. That's as healthy a doughboy foot as I've seen. Dress your foot again, and put on your legging——*pronto*."

A "doughboy" is an infantry soldier. "Pronto" is a word the Army has borrowed from the Spanish, and means, "Be quick about it."

"I'm not fit to march, sir," cried Sergeant Mock.

"Either you'll be ready by the time B company is here, and you'll march in, or I'll detail a man to remain here with you, and send an ambulance for you. If I have to send an ambulance I'll have you examined at the hospital, and if I find you've been faking foot trouble then you shall feel the full weight of military law. I'll give you your own choice. Which do you want?"

Tugging his sock on, Mock merely mumbled.

"Answer me!" Greg insisted sharply.

"I——I'll do my best to march, sir."

"Then be sure you're ready by the time B company gets here, and be sure you march all the way in," Greg ordered sternly. He hated a shamming imitation of a soldier.

Major Bell and his staff came by at the head of the line, followed by Prescott and A company.

"Don't disappoint me, Sergeant," Greg warned his man.

Though his brow was black with wrath Sergeant Mock stood up by the time that the head of B company arrived.

"Take your place, Sergeant," Greg ordered, and waited to see his order obeyed, next running up to his own post.

Ten minutes later, as a group of carpenters from the rifle range paused at the roadside, Greg chanced to glance backward. He was just in time to see Sergeant Mock limping out of the line of file-closers to sit down at the roadside.

His jaws set, Greg Holmes darted back.

"That's enough of this, Mock," he called. "You can't sham in B company. Your feet, I suppose?"

"Yes, sir," groaned the sergeant.

"First two men of the rear four of B company fall out and come here," Captain Holmes shouted.

Instantly the two men detached themselves from the company and came running back.

"Fix your bayonets," Greg ordered. "Bring Sergeant Mock in at the rear of the battalion. If he shirks, prod him with the points of your bayonets. Don't be brutal, but make the sergeant keep up at the rear of the battalion."

"Sir——" began Mock protestingly.

"Quite enough for you, Sergeant Mock," Greg rapped out. "I'll have your feet examined by a surgeon when you come in. Unless the surgeon tells me that I'm wrong you may look for something to happen!"

As Greg turned and started to run back to the head of his company he thought he heard a sound like a hiss. In his opinion it came from some one in the group of carpenters, but he did not halt to investigate.

Though Mock limped all the way in, he came in exactly at the tail of the battalion. As the last company halted on the drill ground Sergeant Lund came back for him, relieving the guards.

"Mock, until you've been examined," said the top, "you're not to go beyond battalion bounds."

"Am I in arrest?" demanded Mock, his face set in ugly lines.

"You're confined within battalion bounds. Remember that," saying which First Sergeant Lund turned and strode away.

Nor was Mock a happy man. Holmes arranged that a regimental surgeon should come over to B company barracks later and make a careful examination of Sergeant Mock's feet. For some reason the surgeon did not come promptly. The evening meal was eaten, and darkness settled down over Camp Berry. Mock, still limping and looking woeful, kept out in the open air.

"Psst!" came sharply from somewhere, and Mock, turning, saw a man in civilian garb standing in the shadow of a latrine shed.

"Come here," called the stranger. Still surly, but urged by curiosity, Mock obeyed the summons.

"I don't want to be seen talking with you," murmured the stranger, in a low voice, "but I want to offer you my sympathy. Say, but a man gets treated roughly in the Army. That captain of yours——"

As the stranger paused, looking keenly at Mock, the disgruntled sergeant finished vengefully:

"The captain? He's a dog!"

"Dog is right," agreed the stranger promptly. "Will he do anything more to you?"

"I expect he'll bust me," said Sergeant Mock.

To "bust" is the same as to "break." It means to reduce a non-com to the ranks.

"Are you going to stand it?" demanded the stranger.

"Fat chance I'll have to beat the captain's game!" declared Mock angrily.

"But are you going to pay him back?"

"How?"

"Listen. I was in the Army once, and I don't like these officer boys. Maybe I've something against your captain, too. Anyway, keep mum and take good advice, and I'll help you to make him wish he'd never been born."

"Not a chance!" dissented Sergeant Mock promptly. "Captain Holmes isn't afraid of anything, and besides he was born lucky. Besides that, do anything to hurt him, and you've got Captain Prescott against you, too, and ready to rip you up the back."

"It's as easy to put 'em both in bad as it is to do it to either," promised the stranger. "Now, listen. You——"

CHAPTER III

BAD BLOOD COMES TO THE SURFACE

Later in the evening the surgeon came around. After examining Sergeant Mock's feet for twenty minutes, and testing the skin as well, he pronounced Mock a shammer.

Mock was sent to the guard-house for twenty-four hours. The next morning an order was published reducing the sergeant to the rank of private. Yet, on the whole, the ex-sergeant looked pleased in a sullen, disagreeable sort of way. He had listened to the stranger.

Greg, however, had other troubles on his hands. After the noon meal that day, as he was on his way to his quarters upstairs Captain Cartwright passed him in the corridor.

"I hear you're turning martinet," said Cartwright, with a disagreeable smile.

"Very likely," smiled Holmes, "but what are the specifications?"

"I heard that you had a sergeant busted for having an opinion of his own."

"That's not so," Greg declared promptly.

"Do you mean to tell me I'm a liar?" Cartwright asked flushing.

"Did I understand you to charge me with preferring unjustifiable charges against a sergeant in my company?"

"I said I heard you had busted a sergeant for doing his own thinking," the other captain insisted.

"Cartwright, it's difficult for me to guess at what you're driving," Holmes went on, patiently, "but I've already told you that I did nothing of the kind that you allege."

"That's calling me a liar again!" flamed Cartwright.

"I'm sorry if it is," returned Greg coolly, and turned toward his door.

"You cannot call me a liar!" cried Captain Cartwright, taking a quick step forward, his fists clenched.

"Apparently I don't have to," scoffed Holmes. "You're eager to claim the title for yourself."

Up flew the other captain's fist. But just then a door opened behind him, and Dick Prescott caught the uplifted fist in tight, vise-like hold.

"Don't do that, Cartwright," he advised.

"Let me alone," insisted the other striving though failing to release his captured wrist.

"Don't do anything rash, Cartwright. Listen to good sense; then I am going to let go of your wrist. If you were to strike Holmes he would be practically bound to thrash you, or else to prefer charges. In either case the matter would get before a court-martial. My testimony, from what I overheard, would have to sustain Holmes."

"You two would swear for each other anywhere and at all times," sneered Captain Cartwright.

This was hinting that Dick Prescott would be willing to perjure himself, and Dick flushed, though with difficulty he kept his patience.

"I'm going to let go of you now, Cartwright," Prescott continued.

As Dick let go of the captured wrist Captain Cartwright wheeled and aimed a vicious blow at his brother officer's face.

But Prescott's arm thrust up his adversary's.

"Stop it, Cartwright!"

Apparently the other could not control his anger. He aimed another savage blow. Dick parried with a thrust, but this time his other fist landed on Cartwright's chest with force enough to send him staggering to a fall on the floor.

At this moment a step was heard on the stairway.

"Gentlemen! Stop this! What does it mean?"

The voice was full of authority and outraged dignity. Colonel Cleaves, his eyes flashing, stood before them.

"Get up, Captain Cartwright," he commanded. "I must have an instant explanation of this scene. Officers and gentlemen cannot conduct themselves like rowdies."

Captain Cartwright forced himself to smile as he saluted; he even tried to look forgiving.

"A little frolic, sir," he made haste to say, "that developed into bad blood for the moment." I do not wish to prefer any charges."

"Do you, Captain Prescott?" demanded the colonel.

"No, sir."

"You, Captain Holmes?"

"No, sir."

If any of the trio had hoped this much explanation would prove satisfactory to the E.O. of the Ninety-ninth, that one had reckoned without his host.

"A misunderstanding that develops to the point of a knock-down blow is never a trifling matter," declared Colonel Cleaves. "If you gentlemen had assured me that it was all frolic then I would have thought no more of it. But I have been assured that there was a misunderstand——a quarrel that proceeded to blows. And I myself saw one man down and signs of very evident anger on all your faces. Gentlemen, do you wish to offer me any further explanation at this moment?"

"I have said all that I really can say, sir," protested Cartwright, "except that I do not harbor any unkind feelings for what has taken place."

Steps were heard on the stairs, and other officers of the Ninety-ninth came upon the scene.

"As no charges have been preferred," said Colonel Cleaves, "I will not order any of you relieved from duty. I will notify all three of you, however, at a later hour, and will then hear you all in my office. I trust a most satisfactory explanation all around will be forthcoming."

Colonel Cleaves then turned to the group of officers that had just arrived, saying:

"Lieutenant Terry, you were kind enough to offer to loan me a book on rifle range construction. I am aware that you have not yet had a chance to send it over to me, but as I was passing, I decided to drop in and ask it from you."

"In an instant, sir," replied Noll Terry. Saluting, he darted down the corridor, opened his door and came back with the volume.

"I am indebted to you, Mr. Terry," said Colonel Cleaves, returning the first lieutenant's second salute and turning to go.

Until they had heard the colonel go out upon the steps below the entire group of younger officers stood as though spell-bound. But at last one of them broke out with:

"I hope nothing really nasty is afoot. Three of you look as though the moon were clouded with mischief for some one."

"You'll pardon us, won't you?" smiled Dick pleasantly, as he turned to go back into his quarters. "You will realize, as we do, that the first discussion of the matter should take place before the commanding officer."

Greg followed his chum in.

"Oh it's nothing," they heard Captain Cartwright assure the others. "It ought to blow over, and I hope it will. A certain officer took what I thought too much liberty with me, and when I resented it his friend took a hand in the matter. I hope we can set it all straight before Colonel Cleaves."

Behind the closed door, hearing what was said, Prescott turned on his friend with eyebrows significantly raised. Greg nodded. No word was spoken.

Apparently Captain Cartwright also went to his quarters, for the steps of many sounded outside, and then all was still.

Prescott had picked up a book and was reading. Greg walked over to the window and stood looking out into the sun-baked company street.

"I must go over to company office for an hour or so," announced Captain Dick, glancing at his wrist watch and laying down his book at last. "After that I'll go out and see how the platoon commanders are getting along with their new work. I hear that we're to have some drafts of new men to-morrow."

"Yes," Greg nodded. "Recruits from Chicago, and also from Boston. Some day we may hope to have our companies filled up to full strength."

"Small chance to get over to France until our companies are filled," Prescott smiled, as he stood up, looked himself over and started for the door.

Captain Greg Holmes followed at his heels. No word was spoken of the recent trouble with Cartwright, not even when they crossed the road below and started for their respective company offices.

Paper work engrossed Prescott's attention for an hour or so. During this time he occasionally glanced up to note what was taking place beyond the window in front of his desk. His four second lieutenants were in command of the platoons to-day, instead of sergeants. The young officers were instructing their men in the first essentials of bayonet combat.

The last piece of paper disposed of, Prescott at last arose, stretched slightly, then strode out of the office to the drill ground.

He was just in time to hear one of his lieutenants explaining to a line of men:

"When pursuing a retreating enemy one of the most effective thrusts with the bayonet can be delivered right here. Learn to mark the spot well."

Half-turning, the lieutenant pointed to the spot in the small of his own back, before he went on, impressively:

"A bayonet thrust there will drive the blade through a kidney. I will admit that that doesn't sound like sportsman-like fighting, but unfortunately we're not to be employed against a really civilized enemy in this war. Page, you will stand out. It isn't a popular role to which I am going to assign you, but you will run slowly past me and represent a fleeing enemy. Dobson, you will take a blob-stick and chase Page, running just fast enough to overtake him in front of me. Then you will give him the kidney thrust, taking care to make your aim exact. Thrust with spirit, but do not hit hard, even with the blob-stick, for Page is not a real German."

Though the men were perspiring uncomfortably, their officer's pleasant conversational way and his interesting talk kept the interest of these young soldiers. Private Page stepped out and took post where the lieutenant indicated, prepared to begin running away at the word of command. Private Dobson picked up a blob-stick, a long, wand-like affair intended to represent a rifle and bayonet, the bayonet's point being represented by a padded ball such as is seen on a bass drummer's stick.

"Go ahead, Page," commanded the lieutenant. "Kill him, Dobson! ... Good work! Any enemy, struck like that in earnest, could safely be left to himself. Dobson, you be the fleeing enemy this time. Aldrich, take the blob-stick."

One after another the men of the skeletonized platoon took their try with the blob-stick. As is usual in the run of human affairs, some of the men made the thrust excellently, others indifferently, and some missed altogether.

"Rest," ordered the lieutenant, presently, and the men stood at ease in the platoon line.

"Some of you men do not get hold of this bayonet work as well as I could wish," Dick spoke up, all eyes turned on him. "The man who learns his bayonet work thoroughly has a reasonably good chance of coming back from Europe alive. The man who learns it indifferently has very little chance of seeing his native land at the close of the war. Remember that. Bayonet fighting is one of the things no American soldier can afford to be dull about. Lieutenant Morris, if you will pick up a blob-stick we can show these men some of the value of swift work in the simpler thrusts and parries."

Each armed with a blob-stick, captain and second lieutenant faced each other. Dick, scowling as though facing an enemy whom he hated, advanced upon his subordinate, making a swift, savage lunge aimed at the other's abdomen. In a twinkling the thrust had been parried by Lieutenant Morris, who, at close quarters, aimed a vicious jab at his captain's wind-pipe. That, too, was blocked. Warming up, the two officers fought without victory for a full three-quarters of a minute. Then, at a word from Prescott, each drew back.

"Every one of you men, by the time you reach France, should be able to fight faster and better than that," Dick announced.

Down the line an infectious smile ran. It seemed to these soldiers impossible that a more skillful or a swifter bit of combat work could be put up than they had just witnessed.

"You two men, at the right, bring your rifles here," Prescott ordered, and the bayoneted rifles were brought and handed to the two officers.

"Now, Lieutenant Morris, the first four series, as fast as we can go through them," Dick commanded.

Bang! bump! flash! Rifle barrels rang as they crossed; butts bumped hard against barrel or stock, and glittering steel flashed in the sunlight as the two infantry officers advanced and retreated in a savage, realistic contest. It really seemed as though Lieutenant Morris and Captain Prescott were bent on annihilating each other. Could this fierce, mutual onslaught be pretense— play? Then, as the last move of the fourth series was executed the two infantry officers jumped back a step each and dipped the points of their gleaming blades by way of courtesy. The other three platoons of the company had stopped drill to watch. How the thrilled men of A company wished to applaud and cheer!

"Lieutenant Morris and I are very poor hands at bayonet work, compared with what we want you men to be when this regiment sails for France," Prescott remarked, smilingly, as he handed back the rifle to its owner.

From that platoon Prescott passed on to others in his company, offering a remark here and a word of instruction there.

"You men must do everything to get your muscles up to concert pitch," Captain Prescott announced. "No lady-like thrusts will ever push a bayonet into a German's face. A ton of weight is needed behind every bayonet thrust or jab!"

An orderly approached, saluting.

"Compliments of the commanding officer, sir, and he will see the captain in his office at regimental headquarters, sir."

Returning the salute Dick walked off the drill ground as though he had nothing on his mind. Down the street he espied Greg, also going toward headquarters, and hurried after him. On the other side of the street was Captain Cartwright, who soon crossed over to join them.

In silence, the three captains made their way along the street until they reached regimental headquarters. It was a low one-story pine shed, with the colonel's office at one end, the adjutant's office next to it, and beyond that the rooms occupied by the sergeant major and his clerical force, and, last of all, the chaplain's office.

None of the three captains was exactly at ease as they entered the adjutant's office and reported.

"The commanding officer will see you at once," said the adjutant. "Pass through into his office."

Colonel Cleaves, glancing up from his desk, gravely returned the salutes of his three captains.

"Be good enough to close the door into the adjutant's office, Captain Holmes," directed the K.O. "Now, gentlemen, I will hear whatever explanation you have to offer of a very remarkable scene that I came upon this noon."

All three waited, to see if one of the others wished to speak first. After waiting a moment or two Colonel Cleaves asked:

"Captain Prescott, it was you who struck the knock-down blow, was it not?"

"Yes, sir," Dick answered promptly, "though it followed a parry, and was more of a thrust than a blow."

"You agree to that, Captain Cartwright?" quizzed the K.O.

"Essentially so, sir."

"There had been a quarrel, had there not?"

"I made a reply to a remark by Captain Cartwright, sir," Greg supplied, "which, he felt justified in construing as offensive, though I did not so intend it. I was annoyed at what I felt to be an insinuation. Then Captain Prescott came out of his quarters, sir, and caught Captain Cartwright's wrist. When Captain Prescott released it, Captain Cartwright struck at him. The blow was parried, and Captain Cartwright struck once more. That blow was also parried, and Captain Cartwright went to the floor."

"Do you concur in that, Captain Cartwright?" asked the K.O.

"Yes, sir."

"By the way, Captain Prescott," went on Colonel Cleaves, handing him a small piece of paper, "can you account for this?"

As Dick Prescott took the paper and glanced at it he felt himself turning almost dizzy in bewilderment.

CHAPTER IV

"That is your handwriting, is it not, Captain Prescott?" demanded the regimental commander.

"It looks just like my handwriting, sir, but I'll swear that I never wrote it," declared astonished Dick, still staring at the little piece of paper.

"Yet it resembles your handwriting?"

"Yes, sir. If I didn't know positively that I didn't write any such message then I'd be about ready to admit that it is my handwriting. But I didn't write it, sir."

"Pass it to Captain Holmes. I will ask him if he has seen this note before."

"No, sir," declared Greg, very positively, though he, too, was startled, for it was hard to persuade himself that he was not looking down at his chum's familiar handwriting.

The note read:

"Dear H. Stick to what we agreed upon, and we can cook C's goose without trouble. P."

"May I speak, sir?" asked Dick.

"Yes, Captain."

"Then I desire to say, sir, that I have not the least desire to see Captain Cartwright in any trouble. Hence, it would have been impossible for me to think of writing such a note. More, sir, it would have been stupid of me to risk writing such a note, for Captain Holmes and I sat in my quarters until it was time for us to leave on our way to our respective company offices."

"And while in your quarters did you discuss this affair of your trouble with Captain Cartwright?"

"To the best of my recollection, sir, we did not mention it," Dick declared.

"Is that your recollection, Captain Holmes?"

"Yes, sir."

"And this is not your handwriting, Captain Prescott?"

"I give you my word of honor, sir, that I did not write it, and did not even discuss the matter with Captain Holmes."

"I do not understand this note in the least," Colonel Cleaves went on. "Of course, Captain Prescott, I am bound to accept your assurance that you did not write this. I do not know how the note came here; all I know about it is that I found it on my desk, under a paper weight, about fifteen minutes ago, when I came in."

"It is the work of some trouble-maker, sir," Greg ventured.

"Do you know anything about this note, Captain Cartwright?"

"No, sir," replied that officer, flushing at the intimation that he could have had anything to do with it, for Greg had passed the paper to him.

"I will keep that note, then," said Colonel Cleaves, taking it, "in the hope that I may later find out how it came to be here. Captain Cartwright, do you deny that Captain Prescott did no more than to parry your blows and thrust you back off your balance?"

"That was all he did, sir."

"And you made two distinct efforts to hit him?"

"Y-y-yes, sir."

"Was anything said that, in your opinion, justified you in attempting to strike a brother officer?"

"At the time I thought Captain Holmes had justified my attempt to \ strike him."

"Do you still think so?"

"N-no, sir. I was undoubtedly too impetuous."

"And you attempted to strike Captain Prescott only because he tried to restrain you from striking a brother officer?"

"Yes, sir."

"Is there anything more to be said or explained by any of you gentlemen?"

"Nothing, sir," came from three pairs of lips.

"Then, since none of you wishes to prefer charges," pursued Colonel Cleaves, "I will say that the whole affair, as far as it has been explained to me, looks like a childish quarrel to have taken place between officers and gentlemen. On the statements made to me, I will say that I believe that Captain Cartwright was most to blame. I therefore take this opportunity to rebuke him. Captain Prescott, of course, you understand that I accept your assurance that you did not write the note I showed you. Keep the peace after this, gentlemen, and make an honest effort to promote brotherliness of spirit with all the officers of the service, and especially of this regiment. That is all."

Saluting, the three captains stepped out into the sunlight. The sentry pacing on headquarters post swung his rifle from shoulder arms down to port arms, then came to present arms before the officers, who acknowledged his formal courtesy by bringing their hands up smartly to the brims of their campaign hats.

"Well, that's over!" announced Cartwright, in a tone of relief.

"And will never be repeated," said Greg.

"But you will admit, Holmes, that you've picked a good deal on me, from time to time," Cartwright pressed, in a half-aggrieved tone.

"I will admit, for you both," smiled Dick, "that you're in danger of starting something all over again unless you shut up and make a fresh, better start. So we won't refer to personal matters again, but we come to your company's barracks first, Cartwright, and when we get there we will shake hands and agree to remember that we're all engaged in a fierce effort to make the Ninety-ninth the best American regiment."

In silence the three pursued their way to C company's building.
Here they halted.

"To the Ninety-ninth, best of 'em all," proposed Prescott, holding out his hand to Cartwright, who took and pressed it.

"To the best officers' crowd in the service," quoth Greg.

"Amen to that!" assented Cartwright, though he strode away with a dull red flush burning on either cheek.

Half an hour later Dick's business took him past the regiment's guard-house. As carpenters were everywhere busy in camp putting up more necessary buildings the place officially known as the guard-house was more of a bullpen. Posts had been driven deeply in the form of a rectangle, and on these barbed wire had been laid to a height of nine feet. Within the rectangle guard-house prisoners could take the air, retiring to either of two tents inside the enclosure whenever they wished.

As he passed Dick noted, vaguely, that four or five men stood by the nearer line of barbed wire fence. He held up his left hand to glance at his wrist watch. Just as he turned the hand, to let it fall at his side, something dropped out of the air, falling squarely in his hand. Instinctively Prescott's fingers closed over the missile. He glanced, quickly, at the enclosure, but not one of the men on the other side of the wire was looking his way.

Then the young captain, keeping briskly on his way, opened his hand to glance down at his unexpected catch. It was a piece of manila paper, wrapped around a stone.

Waiting only until he was some distance from the bull-pen, Dick unwrapped the paper.

In printed characters, used undoubtedly to disguise handwriting, was this message:

"Watch for all you're worth the carpenter who talks with Mock!"

"Now, why on earth should I interest myself in the affairs of Greg's busted sergeant?" Dick wondered. "And what possible interest can I have in any carpenter unless he's a friend of mine, or has business with me?"

On the whole Prescott felt that he was lowering his own dignity to attach any importance to an anonymous message, plainly from a guardhouse prisoner. Yet he dropped the small stone and thrust the scrap of paper into a pocket for future consideration should he deem it worth while.

CHAPTER V

THE CAMP CARPENTER'S TALE

After a week of exacting office work and all but endless drill, Dick had the rare good fortune to find himself with an evening of leisure.

"Going to be busy to-night?" Dick asked Greg at the evening meal at mess.

"Confound it, yes," returned Captain Holmes. "I must put in the time until midnight with Sergeant Lund going over clothing requisitions for my new draft of men."

"My requisitions are all in, and I expect the clothing supplies to-morrow morning," Dick continued.

"That is because you got your draft of new men two days earlier than I did," grumbled Greg. "You're always the lucky one. But what are you going to do to-night that you want company?"

"I thought I'd like to take a walk in the moonlight," Dick responded.

"Great Scott! Do you mean to tell me you don't get enough walk in the daytime in the broiling sunlight?"

"Not the same kind of walking," Prescott smiled. "I want to stroll to-night and talk. But if I must go alone, then I shall have to think."

"Don't attempt hard work after hours," advised Holmes.

"Such as walking?"

"No; thinking."

Dick finished his meal and stepped outside in the air. The first to join him was Lieutenant Morris.

"Feel like taking a walk in the moonlight?" Dick asked.

"I'd be delighted, Captain, but to-night I'm officer in charge at the company barracks."

"True; I had forgotten."

Other officers Dick invited to join him, but all had duty of one kind or another, or else home letters to write.

"Did I hear you say you were going to take a walk, Prescott?" asked Major Wells.

"Yes, sir. By any great good luck are you willing to go with me?"

"I'd like to, Prescott, but as it happens there is the school for battalion commanders to-night. A talk on trench orders by the brigadier is listed, I believe."

"I'm afraid I shall have to go alone," sighed Dick "Yet I've half a mind to stroll over to company office and invent some new paper work. With every one else busy I feel like the only slacker in the regiment."

"If you really go alone," suggested the major, "perhaps you could combine pleasure with doing me a favor."

"How, sir?"

"My horse hasn't had any exercise for three days. I'd be glad if you'd take him out tonight, if it suits you."

"Nothing could please me better, sir," Dick cried eagerly, for he dearly loved a horse.

"How soon will you be ready?"

"At once, Major."

"Then I'll send around now for the horse." Just a few minutes later an orderly rode up, dismounted, saluted and turned the saddled animal over to A company's commander.

"This is luck, indeed!" Dick told himself, as he felt the horse's flanks between his knees and moved off at a slow canter. "I wonder why I never tried to transfer into the cavalry."

While waiting for the horse he had telephoned the adjutant, stating that for the next three hours he would be either in camp or in the near vicinity.

After being halted by three outlying sentries Prescott rode clear of the camp bounds, riding at a trot down a moonlit country road. Vinton was the nearest town, where soldiers on a few hours' pass went for their recreation out of camp. The road to Vinton was usually well sprinkled with jitney busses conveying soldiers to or from camp, so Prescott had chosen another road which, at night, was likely to be almost free of traffic of any kind.

"As this is the first evening I've had off in three weeks I don't believe I need feel that I'm loafing," Dick reflected. "It's gorgeous outdoors to-night. There will undoubtedly be plenty of moonlight in France, but there won't be many opportunities like this one."

Finding that his horse was sweating, Dick slowed the animal down to a walk. He had ridden along another mile when, near a farmhouse he espied a soldier in the road, strolling with a young woman.

As the horse gained upon the young couple the soldier glanced backward, then swung the girl to the side of the road and halted beside her, drawing himself up to attention and saluting smartly. The man was Private Lawrence of his own company.

"Good evening," Dick nodded, pleasantly.

"Good evening, sir," replied the private.

Dick didn't ask, as some officers would have done, whether the soldier had pass to be out of camp. He could ascertain that on his return to camp. Instead, he said:

"You must have this road pretty nearly to yourself, Lawrence, as far as soldiers go."

"There's at least one other, sir," the soldier replied, in a matter of fact way. "I saw one slip by in the field, close to the road. I won't be sure, but I think it was Private Mock, sir."

"He has friends down this way?" Dick asked casually.

"Not that I ever heard of, sir. There aren't many houses on this road. My friend, Miss Williams, lives in the house up yonder."

At the implied introduction Prescott raised his campaign hat, then rode on.

The instant that Mock's name had been mentioned it had flashed through Dick's mind that, when in Greg's office that afternoon, he had seen Mock's name on Top Sergeant Lund's list of men for pass, and Greg, he knew, had drawn a pen line through that name.

"Of course it may not have been Mock that Lawrence saw; Lawrence himself wasn't sure," Dick reflected. "Yet, if Mock is out of camp to-night he is out without leave. Private Lawrence didn't realize that, or he wouldn't tell tales."

Soon the horse began to move along an up grade road between two lines of trees. Finding that the animal, instead of drying off, was sweating more freely, Dick drew rein and dismounted.

"It's hard work on a hot night, so you and I will walk together for a while, old pal," Dick confided to the borrowed mount. "There, you find it easier, don't you?"

As if to express gratitude the horse bent its head forward, rubbing against Dick's shoulder.

"Who says horses can't talk plainly, hey, old fellow?" Dick demanded. On together they walked, until Prescott felt himself perspiring, while the horse's coat grew dry.

"There, now, friend," said Dick, running a hand over the creature's flanks, "you're cool and dry, and this is one of the prettiest spots in Georgia, so I reckon I'll tie you and rest until I, too, am dry again."

Having tied the horse by the bridle reins, Dick strolled about, enjoying the dark and quiet after the bright electric lights and the bustle of camp. Presently he strolled down the road until he came to a break in the trees on his right. Though the moon had gone partly behind a cloud Dick found himself gazing down a clearing. He would not have been interested, had it not been that he caught sight of the unmistakable silhouette of a soldier, and, beside him, a somewhat stoop-shouldered man in darker garb.

"Why, I wonder if that can be Mock, and his carpenter?" reflected Prescott, recalling the note that had dropped so mysteriously into his extended palm.

Screened behind a bush Dick watched the pair until he saw them coming toward the road. Then Prescott drew back, finding better shelter, but he did not seek complete concealment. It occurred to him to wait there, in silence, and see if Private Mock displayed any uneasiness on coming face to face with his captain's chum.

"That will be a good way, perhaps, to test out the note," Prescott decided.

Though the two men appeared to be talking earnestly, only a mumble of voices reached Dick's ears when the men were no more than thirty feet away. Then they stepped into the road, where they halted hardly more than a dozen feet away from the screened captain.

"It's a pity you wouldn't have your nerve," said the stranger, to Mock. "You tell me you hate your captain."

"Wouldn't you, if he had treated you like he treated me?" demanded Mock heatedly.

"Surely I would," agreed the stranger.

"And there's Holmes's friend, that fellow Prescott, who, he, you say, would spend all his time looking into anything that happened to Holmes. You could settle with them both, and then there'd be no one left to worry about."

"Say, just what are you thinking of doing to 'em?" demanded Mock, in a tone of uneasy suspicion.

"There are two things that could be done to them," continued the civilian. "One would be to put them out of the way altogether, and the other would be to bring disgrace upon them so that they'd be kicked out of the Army. That would break their hearts, wouldn't it?"

"Yes," muttered Mock, "but you're talking dreams, neighbor. I'm no black-hander, to creep up behind them with a knife, or take a pot shot at them. I'm not quite that kind, neighbor, and it couldn't be done, anyway."

"You could put 'em out of the way, and no one would be the wiser," hinted the stranger.

"How?"

"I'll show you, when I'm sure enough that you're game," declared the civilian. "I'd have to be sure you had the nerve."

"I haven't," admitted Private Mock.

"Do you know, I began to think that before you admitted it?" sneered the other.

"Not the way you mean," flared up the ex-sergeant. "I can be mean in order to get square with a mean officer. But I can get along without putting him under the sod. I'm a good hater, but my mother didn't raise me to be a real crook."

"You're a quitter, I guess," jeered the other. "Anyway, if you claim to be a man of sand you'll have to show me."

"And I guess it's about time that you showed me something, too," challenged Mock, looking furtively at the stoop-shouldered man.

"I'm ready enough to show you a whole lot of things, when I find out that you're man enough to stand up for yourself and pay back those who treat you like dirt," retorted the other.

"There's one thing you can show me, first of all," challenged Mock.

"Yes? What?"

"Show me why you're so anxious to have harm happen to Captain Holmes and Captain Prescott."

"Because I like you; because I'm a friend of yours," returned the stoop-shouldered one.

"You're a pretty new friend," Mock went on. "I never saw you until that day when the captain caught me shirking and told off two men to prod me back into camp."

"That was the time for you to know me," declared the other brazenly. "That was the time when you needed a friend to show you how to get square like a man instead of like a coward and a quitter."

"Be careful with your names!" commanded Mock harshly. "Say, Mr. Man, who are you, and what are you?"

"Private Mock, I believe I can answer that question for you!" broke in Captain Dick Prescott, stepping out from behind his leafy screen.

CHAPTER VI

"Captain Prescott!" uttered Mock, starting back in dismay.

"Donner und blitzen!" (thunder and lightning) ejaculated the stoop-shouldered one.

"The fellow has just answered your question for you," Dick went on, pointing an accusing finger at the stranger. "You know what language he was betrayed into using just now."

"German, sir," said Mock.

"That's right," nodded Prescott.

"Is he one of them Kaiser-hound spies, sir?" demanded Mock, stung to wrath and throwing grammar to the winds. "Why, I've dreamed of catching one and tearing him to pieces. With your permission, sir———-!"

Not stopping to finish Mock threw himself upon the stoop-shouldered one, But that worthy had foreseen it, and adroitly stopped the ex-sergeant with a blow on the end of the nose that dazed him for an instant.

"I'll take care of him, Mock!" cried Captain Dick, leaping forward. As he did so the stranger turned and fled. No longer stoop-shouldered, but bearing himself like an athlete, the unknown turned and darted away, Prescott racing after him.

"Get back!" warned the fugitive, drawing an automatic revolver and flourishing it over his head.

Though unarmed, save for his fists, Prescott continued to pursue with all speed. After both of them raced Private Mock.

Dick was gaining when he stepped on a round stone, slipped and fell. Mock dashed after him. The fleeing German halted long enough to hurl the automatic pistol at Mock's face, then turned and ran on. Naturally the soldier dodged the missile, which struck the ground behind him. Thinking the weapon might be useful, Mock halted, then ran back and secured the pistol, after which he started to give chase. But the fugitive had vanished in the darkness.

"Come back here and surrender, before I shoot," bluffed Mock, but the German did not answer.

To Mock's intense astonishment Dick reached over, snatching the pistol from his hand.

"That will be about all, Private Mock," said Prescott sternly. "You've bluffed your part well, and helped your friend to escape, but at all events I've got you!"

"Do you——" began the soldier, but stopped, further words failing him. Dick gripped the man's arm, giving a significant pressure before he said:

"You'll come along with me, Mock, and it will be worse for you if you try any further monkey-shines with me."

He gave another pressure on Mock's arm as he finished. Without a word Mock walked with him to where the horse was tied.

"Untie that bridle and buckle the ends together," Dick ordered.

This done, the captain mounted, taking the bridle in his left hand, retaining the automatic pistol in his right.

"March ahead, Mock. Don't try to bolt unless you want me to shoot."

In this manner they proceeded back over the road. Mile after mile they covered, meeting no one until they had come in sight of the camp, nestling in the broad valley below.

At this point such an extensive view could be had that Dick felt sure there was no eavesdropper. So he dismounted, calling the soldier to him and asking in a whisper:

"Mock, you were simply a poor, shirking soldier, weren't you?
You are, at heart, loyal to your country's Flag, aren't you?"

"I'd die for the Stars and Stripes, sir!" Mock declared, in a voice choked with emotion.

"But I felt tired, the other day, and I got a notion Captain Holmes was down on me. So I went bad and got busted. Then I hated Captain Holmes, sir, and ached for a chance to get square with him. Then that accursed carpenter fellow hunted me out, talked with me, and made me think he was my friend. If I had known he was a Kaiser-hound I'd have split his head open at the first crack out of the box."

"I didn't doubt you as a loyal man, Mock," Dick continued, in a whisper. "I spoke to you the way I did back on the road because I was sure the fellow was near and listening. I didn't care much about catching him to-night because I hope to catch him later on, and get him even more red-handed. Mock, you're loyal, and I'm going to put your loyalty, if you consent, to a hard, bitter test."

Dick went on in an even lower tone, Mock listening in growing astonishment, without replying a word, though he nodded understandingly.

"So, now," Prescott wound up, "I'm going to continue into camp with you still a prisoner and be mighty hard on you. However, I won't hold the pistol on you any longer."

Into camp Dick marched the soldier, then over toward the buildings of the Ninety-ninth, and thence along to the bull-pen.

"Sergeant of the guard!" Prescott called briskly, and that non-commissioned officer appeared.

"Take charge of Private Mock as a prisoner, charged with being absent from camp without leave or pass," Dick ordered. "I will report my action to Captain Holmes, who will dispose of his case."

From there Dick led the horse back to B company barracks, turned the animal over to an orderly and went into the company office, where, as he had expected, he found Greg immersed in a grind of paper work. For a few minutes Dick talked earnestly with his chum in low tones, Captain Holmes frequently nodding.

"And now, I think I had better go down to the adjutant's office, to see if he's still at his desk," Dick finished, "and, if so, make my report."

"You'll stagger him," Greg predicted.

One of Greg's orderlies had already ridden the major's horse to the stable, so Prescott walked briskly along the street until he came to regimental headquarters. As he entered the adjutant's office he found Colonel Cleaves seated on the corner of his subordinate's desk, in low-toned conversation with his subordinate.

"Am I intruding, sir?" Dick inquired, saluting the colonel.

"No," said Colonel Cleaves. "In fact, Captain, you may as well know the subject-matter of our conversation. Captain Prescott, this camp would appear to be infested with German spies! This evening sixteen men in F company were taken ill after supper. They are now in hospital and some of them are expected to die. The surgeons have examined some of the food left over from that supper and report finding ground glass in some pieces of the apple pie served as dessert. Later the captain of our machine-gun company, which has only one machine gun so far, had the piece taken into the company mess-room to demonstrate the mechanism to his lieutenants so that they might instruct the men. He found the mechanism of the piece so badly jammed that the machine gun refused to work. I have inspected that piece, and in my opinion the gun is ruined. As if that were not enough sixteen rifles belonging to G company have been found with their bolts broken off. It is very plain that German spies and sympathizers are at work in Camp Berry, and the scoundrels must be found, Captain."

Colonel Cleaves spoke under the stress of great excitement, his eyes flashing, the corners of his mouth twitching.

Dick went to the door, then to the doors opening into the rooms on either side. Then he came back, saying in a low voice:

"Colonel, I met one of the German spies tonight. Perhaps the ring-leader. If I see him again I shall recognize him and arrest him instantly. Do you see what this is, sir?"

Dick held up the weapon that the carpenter had hurled at Private Mock.

"It is a 45-caliber, United States Government automatic pistol," said Colonel Cleaves.

"Exactly, sir; and the spy I have mentioned had it in his possession. How he obtained it, I do not yet know, but I hope to find out. And now, sir, I will tell you what happened and what action I took."

Thereupon Captain Dick Prescott narrated the amazing adventure of the evening, winding up with:

"So, sir, I have placed Private Mock in arrest at the guard-house, and through his detention there I hope to gain the clues that shall lead us to the ferreting out and arrest of the whole crew of German spies at Camp Berry!"

CHAPTER VII

New barracks buildings continued to spring up at Camp Berry. Drafts of men for a National Army division began to arrive, besides a brigade of infantry, a regiment of field artillery and a machine-gun battalion of regulars.

Brigadier-General Bates arrived to take command of the regulars, while Major-general Timmins assumed command of the National Army division and became commanding general of the camp as well.

New batches of recruits, constantly arriving for the regulars, soon gave the Ninety-ninth an average of a hundred and eighty men to the company, or forty-five men to each platoon. Drill went on as nearly incessantly during daylight as the men could endure.

"In my opinion it won't be very long before the Ninety-ninth goes over and reports to General Pershing," Dick told his chum. "At the rate our ranks are being filled up we'll soon have a full-strength regiment."

"But most of our men are still recruits," Holmes objected. The regiment really isn't anywhere near fit for foreign service."

"It won't be so many weeks before we're ordered abroad," Dick insisted. "Wait and see whether I'm right."

Wonderful indeed was the speed with which buildings were erected. The record time for constructing a two-story building with an office, supply room, mess-room and sleeping quarters for two hundred and fifty men was ninety minutes!

Fast, too, was the work done by the Regular Army regiments, which had this advantage over the National Army regiments, that most of their officers were trained regulars and a large proportion of them West Point graduates.

Of the sixteen men made ill by eating powdered glass not one died, for the glass had been ground too fine to do the utmost mischief. However, the camp was alarmed, and all food was kept under close guard and was regularly examined with care before being served.

Soldiers bearing German names were in some instances suspected, and unjustly. Officers tried to undo this harm by talking among the men. Yet all wondered what would be the next outbreak of spy work in camp.

Private Mock, sentenced to two weeks' arrest for being off the reservation without leave, served his sentence moodily, usually refusing to talk with his fellow-prisoners.

One Private Wilhelm was also serving a term in arrest at the bull-pen. His name was held against him Wilhelm as a brand-new man in the regiment, and one of the few with whom Mock would talk.

One morning the latter was overheard to say:

"I'm sick of this war already. I hope the Germans win. If I'm sent over to France I'll watch my chance to desert and get over to the Germans."

"Oh, ye will, will ye?" demanded Private Riley, another prisoner in the bull-pen. "Ye dir-rty blackguard!"

Buff! The Irish soldier's fist caught Mock squarely on the jaw, sending him squarely to earth, though not knocking him out. After a moment Mock was on his feet again, quivering with rage. He flew at Riley, who was a smaller man, hammering him hard. Other soldier-prisoners interfered on behalf of Riley, whereupon Private Wilhelm, a heavily built fellow, rushed to Mock's aid.

"A German and a German sympathizer!"

With that yell a dozen or so of time prisoners set upon the pair. Some lively and perhaps nearly deadly punishment would have been handed out, had not several men of the guard rushed in, thrusting with their rifle butts and breaking up the unequal fight.

But Mock was reported for his utterance, and Wilhelm for his sympathies. Both were brought up before Captain Greg Holmes, and Dick was sent for to join in questioning the men, which was done behind closed doors. At the end of the hearing Mock and Wilhelm were returned to the guard-house looking much crestfallen.

"Did you hear what they said to me?" Mock was overheard to demand of Wilhelm. "Said they'd have me tried for saying I'd desert, and that I'd be likely to get several years in prison for talking too much. Oh, I'm sure sick of being in this man's army!"

"Sure!" nodded Wilhelm, understandingly. "It's tough!"

"It'll be tougher, I warrant ye, if we hear ye two blackguards using any more of your line of talk around here," Riley broke in. "The guar-rd won't be forever stopping our pounding ye!"

After that Mock and Wilhelm were left severely alone by their fellow-prisoners in the bull-pen. Most of these men were serving merely sentences of a day to a week for minor infractions of discipline.

The next morning Private Riley managed to get word to Greg that Private Brown, of the guard, had been talking with Mock at the barbed wire of the pen enclosure.

"Private Brown is supposed to be an all right soldier, but he'll bear watching," was Dick's comment when he heard the report.

That afternoon it was reported that both Mock and Wilhelm had been talking with Private Brown at the barbed wire fence. Dick smiled grimly when he heard it.

The next morning orders were read releasing Mock, Wilhelm, Riley and some of the other soldier prisoners ahead of time that they might not be deprived of too much instruction. The released ones were cautioned to be extremely careful, in the future, not to fall under the disciplinary ban.

"Sure, I can understand some of us getting out, but not Mock," declared Riley to a bunkie (chum). "Him an' his talk about deserting to the enemy!"

In the meantime Dick had given an accurate description of the carpenter who had tried to enlist Mock in some dangerous scheme of revenge. The fellow had disappeared from among the gang of carpenters, and that was all that was known. Secret Service men had been put on the trail, but had failed to find the fellow.

"Now, maybe a soldier sometimes says more than he means," broke in Sergeant Kelly, who had come up behind the pair on the nearly deserted drill ground. "Soldiers are like other people in that respect."

"But not Mock," Riley objected. "He's a bad egg."

"I don't say he isn't," Kelly rejoined. "What I'm advising you is not to conclude that a man is worthless just because he talks. For that matter, Riley, I believe that the men we have most to fear are spies who manage to get in the Army, talk straight and do their work well, and all the time they're plotting all kinds of mischief. Like the fellow or the chaps who put that powdered glass in the chow of F company not long ago."

"Here's hoping I live to see Mock hanged!" grumbled Private Riley, as Sergeant Kelly moved away.

Kelly, who had served as sergeant with Dick in other regiments, had followed him into the Ninety-ninth. Prescott rejoiced that he had this excellent fellow with him, as capable first sergeants are always looked upon in the light of prizes.

Yet, in a——to him——new man Greg Holmes had an almost equally good top in Lund, a Swede who had put in ten years in the Army.

44

When Greg dropped into the company office that forenoon, Lund handed him a list of men who had put in application for pass that afternoon. It was to be a visitors' afternoon, and there would be no drills.

"Nineteen, and all good conduct men, Sergeant Lund," commented Greg, glancing over the list and reaching for a pencil with which to O.K. the list.

"And two more put in application, but I didn't put their names down, sir," Lund explained, as he stood at the side of the young captain at the desk.

"Who were they?"

"Mock and Wilhelm."

"Have they behaved themselves since they got out of arrest?"

"Oh, yes, sir."

"Then we'll let them off this afternoon," proposed Holmes amiably, as he wrote time two names down on the list. "Perhaps they'll turn out better for a bit of considerate treatment."

Though Lund frowned as he received the list back in his own hand he made no comment.

Immediately after the noon meal Mock and Wilhelm exhibited their passes to the guard and walked briskly out of camp.

"Look at that now——the pair of traitors!" muttered Private Riley, as he spat vengefully on the ground. "Me, I knew better than to ask for it, and me so lately out of the pen. But those bir-rds with dir-rty feathers get their chance to go off the reservation and plot more mischief."

Had Private Riley been able to follow the pair unseen he would have been even angrier. Mock and Wilhelm, stepping briskly along the road over which Dick had ridden that eventful evening, kept on for some three miles, then turned abruptly off into the forest.

For another half mile they kept on, going further and further from the road.

"Here's the spot," said Mock, after some hunting under the trees. "It must be the place, for it has the nail driven into the tree trunk."

"Sure, it's the place all right," Wilhelm agreed.

Mock emitted a shrill whistle that would not, however, carry very far. Instantly there came an answering whistle.

"And here we are!" spoke up the stoop-shouldered stranger, coming out of a. jungle of bushes. "I'm glad to see that you're on time. And to-day I hope you've more sand than you had that night."

"Forget it," said Mock shortly.

"You're ready now?"

"To do anything," Mock agreed.

"Sure! He's all right!" Private Wilhelm nodded. "I've attended to that."

"Come here, Carl!" called the stoop-shouldered one, in a low voice.

From another clump of bushes came another man, bearded and bespectacled. If there's anything in a face, Carl was unmistakably German.

"Carl will tell you what to do," said time stoop-shouldered one.

"You men are in two different companies?" asked the man behind spectacles.

"I'm in B company," nodded Mock. "Wilhelm is in E company."

"Then you can take care of two companies of men," Carl went on. "Do to-morrow morning what I'm going to tell you. See these?"

The bespectacled one held up two vials that he had taken from a pocket.

"Each one of you takes one of these," he went on. "Hide them to-night where you please. In the morning, when the men in your barracks hang their bedding out of the windows and go down to breakfast, stay behind. Uncork a vial, each of you, and sprinkle the liquid in here on the bedding of at least half a dozen soldiers. You understand? Then slip down to your breakfasts."

"What's in these vials?" asked Mock, taking the one offered him and curiously inspecting the liquid in it.

"Germs!" said the bespectacled one. "Measles. Do as I tell you, and in a few days measles will begin to run through the two companies like wildfire. In a few days more it ought to be well through the regiment. Tomorrow night slip out of camp and come here. Under those bushes over there you'll find civilian clothing. Understand? Yes? In the pockets of each suit you'll find the money to pay for your work. Take off your uniforms and put on the other clothes. Then go where you please, but be sure to keep out of time Army after this, for American soldiers are going to die fast! The money you'll find will take care of you. Yes?"

"Yes!" nodded Mock. "Sure!"

Then, suddenly, Mock turned and whistled.

"You two men will throw up your hands!" came in the sharp tones of Captain Dick Prescott, as he, Sergeant Kelly and four privates stepped into view.

"You sneak!" yelled the stoop-shouldered one, making a rush at Mock and trying to seize the vial. But Mock dodged. In the same instant the bespectacled German tried to snatch the other vial away from Wilhelm, but that soldier, too, dodged and saved the vial.

"On the ground is a good place for you!" growled Sergeant Kelly, knocking the stoop-shouldered stranger flat. Then, before the fellow could rise Kelly had snapped handcuffs his wrists.

Two of the soldiers seized the bespectacled German just as he started to run. He, too, felt the clasp of steel around his wrists. Though Kelly and the four privates were armed with automatic pistols no weapon had been drawn.

"Twice you've played the sneak, you!" hissed the stoop-shouldered one, glaring at Private Mock.

"Twice more I'll do it to help Uncle Sam," retorted Mock, with a short laugh. "I owed it to you to see you caught!"

"But you're a German!" hissed the bespectacled one at Wilhelm. "Why did you turn on us, who are also German?"

"My father was a German; he's an American now," said Wilhelm, coolly. "Me, I've always been an American, and I'm one now, and will be as long as I live."

"Let me have those vials," Dick ordered. "Sergeant, take these, and mark them as soon as you get back to company office. Then we'll turn them over to the medical department. Sergeant, march your prisoners."

Heading toward the road Sergeant Kelly and his four soldiers led the German captives away.

Captain Dick, with Mock and Wilhelm, followed, but did not attempt to keep up with the sergeant's party,

When Kelly showed up in camp again he did not have his prisoners with him. He had taken them elsewhere, and they were soon on their way to an internment camp, where, like "good" Germans in America, they would live until the close of the war, cut off from all further chance to plot against Uncle Sam's soldiers.

Halting at a farm-house on the way, Dick telephoned to regimental headquarters. Two minutes after his message had been received Private Brown, white-faced and haggard, was placed under arrest. Under grilling, he confessed what Secret Service men had already learned—that his name was really spelled B-r-a-u-n; that both he and his father were German subjects, and that the young man had enlisted for the sole purpose of playing the spy and the plotter in the Army.

It had been Mock's talk of deserting in France that had caused Braun to talk to Mock, who had been told by Captain Prescott to talk in that vein while in the bull-pen. Braun had fallen into the trap.

As for Wilhelm—which wasn't the young an's real name—he was the son of a German-born father, but a young man of known loyalty to the United States. He wasn't a soldier, but a War Department agent who had donned the uniform for a purpose, and had come to Camp Berry with a draft of real soldiers.

And this was the plan that Dick had worked out following his pretended arrest of Mock that night up the road. Mock, resolved to become a good soldier again, had undergone his humiliation in the bull-pen, and the scorn of his fellow-prisoners, in order to trap the stoop-shouldered German, a pretended carpenter, but really August Biederfeld, a German spy. The bespectacled one, Dr. Carl Ebers, was another spy. The two had delivered their messages in camp through Braun.

While the pair Ebers and Biederfeld were interned, Braun, as one who had enlisted in the Army and had taken the oath of service, was court-martialed on a charge of high treason, and shot for his crimes. Before his death he confessed that it was he who had shaken the powdered glass in the food of F company, the stuff having been supplied by Dr. Ebers. It was Braun, also, who had damaged the machine gun and worked havoc with infantry rifles, he, too, had forged and placed the pretended Prescott note about "Cooking Cartwright's goose."

"Wilhelm" soon vanished, undoubtedly to do other work as an alleged German sympathizer elsewhere. As for Mock:

"Private James Mock, B company, having suffered humiliation and scorn that he might better fulfil his oath and serve his country, is hereby restored to his former rank of sergeant in B company, and with full honor, he will be obeyed and respected accordingly."

So ran the official order published to the regiment.

The liquid in the two vials was found to be swarming with measles germs that would have started a veritable epidemic at Camp Berry.

Captain Dick Prescott's quick thinking and steady action had resulted in the capture of the German spies who were seeking to destroy the Ninety-ninth.

No quiet days, however, were in store for the regiment.

CHAPTER VIII

WITH THE CONSCIENTIOUS OBJECTORS

"No other business, Sergeant?" asked Dick, one October morning, as he looked up from the desk in company office at his "top."

"Among the nineteen National Army men drafted into this regiment, sir, are three conscientious objectors who ask to be transferred to some non-fighting branch of the service."

"Send for them," ordered Dick briefly, a frown settling on his brow.

Privates Ellis, Rindle and Pitson speedily reported in the office, saluting, then standing at attention.

"You men are all conscientious objectors?" Prescott asked coldly.

"Yes, sir," said the three together.

"You all have conscientious objections to being hurt?" Prescott went on.

"I have conscientious scruples against killing a human being, sir," replied Private Ellis.

"And you also have scruples against giving him a chance to kill you," Dick went on mercilessly. "You believe in a police force for preserving order in a community, do you?"

"Y-yes, sir."

"If you found a burglar in your home, and had an opportunity, you would send for a policeman?"

"Yes, sir," Ellis admitted.

"Even though you knew the policeman might find it necessary to kill the burglar in attempting to arrest him?" Prescott quizzed.

"Yes, sir."

"Then, while you presumably would not kill a burglar yourself you would not object to calling a policeman who might do it?"

Private Ellis began to suspect the trap into which he was falling.

"I could not bear to kill the burglar myself, sir," he replied.

"And you would not want the burglar to kill you, so you would summon a policeman to do whatever killing might be necessary. In that case, are you a

49

moral objector to killing, or are you merely a coward who relies on another to do the killing for you?"

Private Ellis appeared much confused.

"Answer me," Dick commanded.

"The case doesn't seem the same to me, sir, as serving as a fighting man in the war."

"The case is exactly the same, except in the matter of magnitude," Prescott retorted. "Germany is the burglar, trying to break into the house of the world. You haven't time necessary courage to fight a German yourself, but you will be glad to see a braver man serve on the firing line in your stead. And you are a conscientious objector, too, are you, Rindle?"

"I——I thought I was, sir," confessed the soldier. "Your questions, sir, and your way of putting the case confuse me."

"And you, Pitson?" Dick demanded, eyeing the third man. "Knowing that, if you are sent to some non-combatant work, some other man will have to be sent to this company to do your killing work for you, you wish to dodge fighting duty?"

"Yes, sir; I do," Pitson answered unhesitatingly.

"Pitson, consider the matter seriously and try to decide whether you're a moral hero or a physical coward!"

"Sir, I am no mor——-"

Here the man hesitated, growing red in the face.

"Out with it," Dick smiled coolly.

"I am a conscientious objector, sir," Pitson rejoined. "No matter what punishment may await me for refusing, I *must* decline to accept any duty that may call upon me to kill another human being."

"Yet you would call a policeman, in the case of finding a burglar in your house?"

"Not if I thought the policeman would have to kill the burglar, sir," Pitson protested.

"I'll wager the fellow is lying, at that," Prescott reflected, as he rose. "Take off your hat, Pitson."

The soldier obeyed. His forehead sloped up and back. The back of his head sloped up and forward, so that the top of his head was pointshaped.

"I've been interested in seeing what the head of a real conscientious objector looked like," Dick remarked slowly. "I've seen your head and from its shape I believe you to be a real conscientious objector. I am going to approve your transfer to a non-combatant branch, Pitson. You may step outside until you are sent for again."

After Pitson had gone Dick ordered the two remaining men to remove their campaign hats. He studied the shapes of their heads so attentively that both young men winced plainly under the inspection.

"Your heads are shaped differently from Pitson's," Prescott went on. "The top of his head goes up to a point. If a mule had a head shaped like that our veterinary surgeons would call it a fool mule and reject it. But you men have heads expressing more intelligence.

"What is the matter with you two? Have you been listening to socialistic or other freak talk? Do you realize that the German Kaiser and his nation threaten the freedom of the world? Do you realize that the Germans want to rule this world, and do you know how they would rule it, and what a miserable, impossible world it would be for free men to live in?

"Do you realize that the only way we can stop the Germans from ruling the world in their own brutal way is for the free men of all good nations to fight? Do you fully understand that we cannot fight such a beastly enemy in any other way than by killing him? Do you so thoroughly object to fighting that you would see a free world ground under the heel of the despotic Kaiser sooner than help kill his soldiers and thus prevent such a world-wide tragedy? Are you men, or are you dish-rags? Are your consciences so important that you would put the world in cruel bondage rather than violate your own little personal ideas of what is moral? Are you men so sure you're right that you'd dodge a slight wrong—-if wrong it be—-and allow the greatest wrong ever attempted to triumph? Do your moral principles tell you that it is better to let Shame rule the world instead of Justice?"

Ellis and Rindle were plainly non-plussed by Dick's passionate appeal to their broader sense of right and truth.

"I'm afraid you two have been patting yourselves on the back in the idea that you stood out for a great moral principle," Captain Prescott resumed. "Don't you begin to see that the fact is that, instead, you're really moral slackers who'd let the world go into the devil's keeping provided you didn't have to be made to do something that you don't want to do? I won't say you're physical cowards, for honestly I hardly think you are, but aren't you at least moral slackers?"

Private Ellis swallowed hard before he replied:

51

"No, sir; I'm not a moral slacker, for I've changed my mind. I'm going to fight if I'm told to. I'm going to do whatever Uncle Sam wants me to do. You've put the matter in a different light to me, Captain Prescott."

"And you, Rindle?"

"I'm going to do myself the honor of asking permission to remain in your company, sir," replied the second man, his mouth twitching. "I'm a bit of a fool, sir. But I don't believe that I'm a fool all the way through. I believe that I can see at least part of a truth when it's put to me fairly, and now I believe that it's right to fight for truth and justice as against black tyranny—-and I'm ready to do it."

"Good enough!" cried Dick, his face lighting up, as he held out his hand. "If you have any further doubts, later, come to me. I don't know everything, but we can get together and perhaps between us we can get close to the truth."

Shaking hands with the soldiers who had found themselves, and dismissing them, Dick added:

"Sergeant Kelly, find out what non-combatant branch that fellow Pitson would prefer to serve in, see what unit will have him, and then bring the transfer papers to me to sign."

Passing into the corridor, and hearing the piano's notes in the mess-room he glanced inside. It was a rest period between drills, and a soldier seated at the instrument strummed his way through the air of a mournful ditty. It's an odd thing that when the average soldier is wholly cheerful he prefers the "sobful" melodies.

At one of the long mess tables near the piano sat four young men, paying no heed to the music, nor, in fact, doing anything in particular.

"How many of you men have mothers?" Prescott asked with a smile.

All admitted that they had.

"How many of you have written that mother to-day?"

None had.

"How many wrote her yesterday?" None.

"Think hard," Dick went on. "Has any of you written his mother a letter within five days?"

One soldier asserted that he had written his mother four days before.

"I wish you men would do me a favor," Dick went on. "Each one of you write his mother at least a four-page letter and mail it before supper. There is going to be time enough between drills to-day. How about it?"

Each of the four soldiers standing at attention promised promptly.

"All right, then," Prescott nodded. "Rest!" Whereupon they resumed their seats on the bench. "Remember that a promise is a promise. And I've seen enough of soldiers to know that they're likely to be careless where it hurts most."

"I'd do anything Captain Prescott asked me to do," remarked one of the soldiers when Dick had passed on out of barracks.

"If I knew anything he wanted me to do I'd do it before he asked me," declared another.

When a captain's men feel that way about him it's a cinch that he commands a real fighting unit.

CHAPTER IX

During the next drill period Sergeant Kelly, hearing an angry voice, glanced out through the window.

In the last draft to the company some green recruits had come in, men who had been drafted to the National Army and sent to the Regulars to fill up. Among them were Privates Ellis and Rindle.

"About face!" rapped out the crisp tones of Corporal Barrow, as he glared at eight men in double rank.

Badly enough most of them turned. "You poor mutt-heads!" rasped the corporal. "Do you think you'll ever make soldiers?"

In a jiffy Kelly reached for his campaign hat, put it on, and stepped out into the corridor, passing out and heading for the drill ground.

"Right dress!" called out Corporal Barrow. "Front! Rotten!
I wonder if you fellows think you'll ever be soldiers?"

Plainly the recruits were chafing under the lash of the corporal's tongue. But Barrow, a young man of twenty-two, who had received his chevrons after only four months of service, was in no mind to be easily pleased to-day.

"You're the most stupid squad in the regiment!" the young non-com went on. "Your place is in the bullpen, not in the ranks."

"Let the squad rest a minute or two, Corporal, and come with me," Sergeant Kelly called placidly. "I've a message far you."

Giving the required order, and lull of curiosity, Corporal Barrow stepped quickly over to Kelly, who, placing a hand on the young man's shoulder, walked him some distance away. Suddenly the top sergeant, his back turned to the squad, grilled Barrow with a blazing gaze.

"You poor boob in uniform!" rapped the sergeant. "Whatever made you think of taking up soldiering. And what made you think yourself fit to be in a regiment of Regulars? Do you know your left foot from your right? You know as much about the manual of arms as I do about Hebrew verbs. When you salute an officer you're a standing disgrace to the service! Do you know what you ought to be doing in life?"

His face growing violently red, Barrow soon forgot to be indignant in the

54

excess of his wonder.

"Meaning—-what?" he demanded, thickly, his lower jaw sagging in bewilderment.

"How do you like the way I'm talking to you?" asked Sergeant Kelly, his own strong jaw thrust out as though he were seeking to provoke a quarrel.

"Why do you ask?" demanded the corporal, with some show of spirit. "Does any man enjoy being spoken to like a thieving dog?"

Instantly Kelly dropped back into a placid tone.

"How do you think the men of that squad like hearing you talk to them as I've just talked to you?"

"But they're such numbskulls!" declared Barrow.

"You won't improve their intelligence by turning the hot water on them all the time," Sergeant Kelly continued. "Could I make a better corporal of you by scorching you every time I saw you?"

"You know you couldn't."

"No more can you turn those rookies into soldiers by raging at them every time you speak. Take it from me, Corporal Barrow, the wise drill-master doesn't use any rough talk once a week, and not even then unless nothing else will answer. Talk to the men right along as I heard you doing, and they won't have a particle of respect for you. That being the case, you cannot teach them anything that it will be worth their while to know. If the captain had heard what I heard you saying to those men he'd put you back in the awkward squad yourself. Patience is the first thing a drill-master needs. Whom do you call the smartest corporal in the company?"

"Corporal Smedley," Barrow answered, without hesitation.

"Right, and he's going to be the next new sergeant. But Smedley is the most patient drill-master in the company. Shall I send him over to show you how to handle a green squad?"

"Don't, Sergeant!"

"All right, then; I won't—-unless you give me new reason to think it necessary," smiled Kelly. Then his hand, still resting on the younger man's shoulder, he walked back to where the squad waited.

"I'll tell you more about it any time you want to know," was Kelly's last statement before he turned away.

"Attention!" called Corporal Barrow briskly. "Saluting is one of the things a new soldier is likely to do badly at first. I'm going to put you through a few minutes of it."

This time Barrow patiently singled out the soldier giving the poorest salute.

"You don't bring your hand up smartly enough," Barrow explained patiently. "Try it again. No; don't bring it up with a jerk. Do it like this——smartly, without jerk. No; that's not right, either. Hold your hand horizontally when it touches your hat-brim. Hold it the way I am doing. Don't be in a hurry to let hand fall, either. When saluting an officer, keep the hand at the hat-brim until he has returned the salute, or you've passed him. There, you have it right now, Rindle. Do it three times more, dropping your hand when I see you and return the salute. That's it. Good work. Try it again, all together. Squad, salute!"

"Well done, Corporal," chimed in the voice of Captain Prescott, who had come up behind the instructor, "Be sure that the squad has drill enough in the salute, for a man is never a really good soldier until he can render a salute smartly. Let the men break ranks, Corporal, and have each man pass me in turn, saluting the best he knows how."

As Captain Dick stood there, receiving and returning the salute of each rookie as he passed, the young company commander noted each man's performance with keen eyes.

"First rate for recruits, Corporal," Prescott said, as he turned away. "Give them daily drill at it, however."

Corporal Barrow gave his own most precise salute as he received his captain's orders. Then he called:

"In double rank, fall in! Mark time, march! Step more smartly, Pelham. Hip, hip, hip! Squad halt! One, two!"

From the corner of the building Dick had paused an instant to glance back. Then he went into the company office.

"I've just been watching Corporal Barrow and his new recruit squad, Sergeant," Dick announced. "The men are doing first-rate for new men. Corporal Barrow is a patient and competent drill-master."

"Yes, sir," Kelly replied, without trace of a smile.

"The patient instructor is the only one who can teach a recruit, Sergeant. If you ever see a non-com in this company losing his temper set him straight at the first chance."

"Yes, sir."

"But don't make the correction in hearing of the squad unless the case is a flagrant one."

"No, sir," Sergeant Kelly promised, his eyes smileless.

"How near is the company to full strength this morning?"

"Only twelve men short, sir. A new draft, coining in on the 4.10 train this afternoon is expected to fill all companies to strength, sir."

Dick Prescott felt a sudden thrill. Filling up the companies of the Ninety-ninth appeared to promise that the regiment would soon be on its way overseas!

"If we get our full strength this afternoon, Sergeant, be sure to have the clothing requisitions for them all in shape by this evening. Then we'll try to draw to-morrow morning."

"Yes, sir."

"And——sergeant!"

"Yes, sir."

"I'm mighty glad that you applied for transfer to this regiment when I was ordered to it. I don't know what I'd do without you."

"Thank you, sir!"

Kelly had sprung to his feet. He now stood at salute as Prescott left the office.

The train due at 4.10 arrived after 8.30 that evening. Twelve new men, assigned to A company, were marched to barracks after ten. No man in the detachment had eaten since early morning. The mess sergeant had coffee and sandwiches ready.

It was midnight when Kelly, with the aid of other non-coms, had the measurements of the new men on paper and his clothing requisition ready. Dick Prescott was on hand to sign as company commander.

At six in the morning first call to reveille sounded from the bugles.

Like the other companies in the regiment A company tumbled out of its cots. Men dressed, seized soap, towels, brushes and combs, and hurried to the wash-room at the rear of barracks. Then back again, the final touches being administered. Outside a bugle blew, calling the men to first formation. Then mess-call caused two hundred and fifty hungry soldiers to file into the mess-room, kits in hand, and line up at the further end for food and hot drink.

At 7.46 Dick Prescott stepped briskly into the company office.

"Sergeant Kelly, have each man carry out his mattress to the incinerator and empty out the straw. Detail men to burn the straw. Have the cots piled at the end of each squad room. At 8.25 turn the company out with barracks bags and dismiss after the bags have been placed. At 8.40 turn out the company in full marching order, with arms and pack, for inspection. As soon as practicable thereafter the men will be turned out again for issue of razors."

"Yes, sir," Kelly replied with a quiver. "Of course you know what it means, Sergeant?"

"The regiment is moving, sir."

"Moving by rail to the point of embarkation, Sergeant. We're——at last we're going over!"

There must have been an eavesdropper outside the office door, for instantly, so it seemed, the news flashed through the building.

"Orders have come!"

"We're going over!"

"*Now!*"

"Stop that cheering, men!" boomed Dick Prescott's voice, as he stepped into the corridor. "This is Georgia, and you'll wake all the sleeping babies in North Carolina."

CHAPTER X

North to an embarkation camp, not to a pier. There passed several days of restlessness and unreality of life.

Final issues of all lacking equipment were made at last. Then, one evening, after dark, the Ninety-ninth once more fell in and marched away, the bandsmen, carrying their silent instruments, marching in headquarters company.

No send-off, no cheering, not even the playing of "The Girl I Left Behind Me."

No relatives or friends to say good-bye! Nothing but secrecy, expectancy, an indescribable eagerness clothed in stealth.

"How do you feel, Sergeant?" Captain Prescott asked, as he and his top stood at the head of A company awaiting the final order that was to set the nearly four thousand officers and men of the Ninety-ninth in motion on the road.

"Like a burglar, sneaking out of a house he didn't realize he was in, sir," Kelly answered.

First Lieutenant Noll Terry shivered; it was impatient uncertainty——nothing else.

Then the order came. The dense column reached the railway, where the sections of the troop train waited. By platoons the men marched into dimly lighted cars. When all were aboard the lights were turned off, leaving Uncle Sam's men in complete darkness, save where a pipe or cigarette glowed.

Despite the eagerness the newness and uncertainty of it all, many of the soldiers dozed unconscious of the talk and laughter of others. Singing was forbidden and non-coms had orders to be alert to stop any unnecessarily loud noises.

Forth into the night fared the sections of the train. How long it was on the rail none of the men had any clear idea. It was still dark, however, when a stop was made and the order ran monotonously along:

"All out!"

Again dim lights were turned on, that men might find all their belongings. Adjusting their packs the platoons of the Ninety-ninth found their way to the ground below.

For once there was no attempt at good military formation. At route step and in irregular columns, the regiment moved forward by platoons. Unknown officers stood along the way to direct, for the regiment's platoon leaders had no knowledge of the way.

Thus a mile or more was covered by a regiment that looked disorganized and spectral in the darkness. Then the aspect changed somewhat. Whiffs of salt air prepared the soldiers. Army trucks were moving on parallel roads or trails. Ahead of them appeared high fences of barbed wire. It looked as though the travelers had come upon a huge bull-pen. There were gates, guarded by military sentries not of the Ninety-ninth.

Through these gates and past the barbed wire filed the marching men.

Further ahead loomed the sheds of a great pier.

With the help of officers who knew the ground the Ninety-ninth found room to fall in for roll call.

"All present or accounted for!"

Then battalion by battalion, a company at a time, the regiment passed on through the dimly lighted pier sheds. On the further side towered the bulwarks of a great ship, with gangways reaching down to the pier.

In some mysterious way order reigned and speed was observed.
Line after line of uniformed men passed up the gangways and vanished.
Lights were on the ship, yet dim enough to be in keeping with the
night's mystery.

Last of all the almost muffled noises of gangways being drawn down on to the piers. Hawsers were cast off. Stealthy tugs hauled the ocean monster out into the stream.

"Off at last!" was felt more than spoken. Then the tugs let go and the ship, outwardly darkened save for the few necessary running lights, moved slowly down stream.

Some venturesome soldiers found their way up on deck.

Above them, on a still higher deck, the shadowy forms of officers were discernible.

The strangeness of the dark sea lay over all. It seemed uncanny, this dark departure from one's native land——the land for which these men were going to fight, to bleed and die!

Yet there was no sense of fear. It was the strangeness that gripped all minds.

Up forward on the spar deck a few enlisted men opened their mouths to sing. The chorus grew in volume and the words rolled up:

"And I don't know where I'm going, but I'm on my way!"

"For I belong to the Regulars. I'm proud to say."

"And I'll do my dooty-ooty, Night or day."

"I don't know where I'm going, But I'm on my way!" Breaking through the words the ship's deep-throated whistle boomed its own notes.

CHAPTER XI

Some days later the same ship steamed steadily through the waters on the further side of the Atlantic.

Nor was the Ninety-ninth alone. Seven other transports were keeping her company, together with a busy, bustling escort of British and American destroyers.

For these American adventurers of to-day were nearing the coast of Ireland.

Whether these transports were to unload their cargoes of human beings and munitions at any port in Great Britain or Ireland few on the transports knew, nor did those few tell others.

Ever since the first morning out there had been daily drills, on every transport, in abandoning ship. A few night drills, too, had been held. Not an officer or man was there but knew his station and his lifeboat in case of disastrous meeting with a submarine.

These had not been the only drills, however. From morning to night platoons had been drawn up on the decks and military drills had been all but incessant while daylight lasted. Especially had the newest recruits been drilled. By this time the latest of them to join the regiment had gained considerable of the appearance of the soldier.

Dick and Greg, sharing the same cabin, had been much together, for on shipboard they had found much leisure. It had been the lieutenants who had drilled the platoons. Captains were but little occupied on shipboard.

On the morning that it became known that the fleet had entered the Danger Zone, Dick and Greg stood on deck to the port of the pilot house. Leaning over the rail they idly scanned the surface of the sea to northward.

"Almost in France, my boy!" Prescott cried eagerly. "Or England!"

"Near enough, yet we may never see either country," returned Captain Holmes, suppressing a yawn, for the sea air, even after a night's rest, made him drowsy.

"Croaker!" laughed Dick.

"I'm not," Greg denied, "and I don't want to croak, either, but who can tell? We are now in the waters where the sea wolves have been busy enough in finding prey."

"So far they haven't proved that they could do much to troopships," Dick declared warmly.

"There always has to be a first time," Holmes retorted.

"All right, then," smiled Prescott. "We're going to be torpedoed. Now, I hope that satisfies you."

"You know it doesn't," Holmes rejoined. "This sea air makes me so sleepy, all the time, that I don't feel as though I could stand any real excitement."

"Being torpedoed would be something to look back upon in later years," Dick observed thoughtfully.

"Yes, if we had any later years on earth in which to look back," Captain Holmes responded.

"Who's this strange-looking creature coming?" Dick suddenly demanded, as he stared aft.

"Captain Craig, the adjutant, of course," Greg answered. "He has his life belt on, and he's stopping to talk to others."

"After he speaks they hurry away," Dick went on. "I understand. All hands are ordered to put on life belts."

And that, indeed, proved to be the message that Captain Craig brought forward with him. Dick and Greg did not have far to go to reach their cabin. In five minutes they reappeared on deck in the bulky contrivances intended to buoy them up in the water should they have the bad fortune to find themselves tossing on the waves.

"This makes the danger seem real," Prescott observed.

"Too blamed real!" grumbled Greg. "We're ordered not to take these belts off, either, until the order is passed, and are told that the order won't be passed to-day, either. Imagine our trying to get close to the dining table to eat in comfort!"

"It may be in the plans that we're not to eat to-day," Captain Dick laughed.

Ahead, on either flank and at the rear, the torpedo-boat destroyers were scouting vigilantly, with gunners standing by ready to fire promptly at any periscope or conning tower of an enemy craft that might be sighted.

"I don't suppose there'll be any band concert this afternoon," said Greg Holmes suddenly and ruefully. "And we have a mighty good band, too. And probably no band concert to-morrow forenoon, either."

"We may not be at sea to-morrow forenoon," Dick suggested.

"Have you been able to figure out at all where we are?" Captain Holmes asked.

"I haven't. I don't know either our course or the speed at which we are traveling. All I am sure of is that we are still out of sight of land. I was told that we are nearing the coast of Ireland, but Ireland is a town of some size, so the information isn't very explicit."

"Say," ejaculated Greg, suddenly looking over at the water, "we have begun to hit up a faster speed. So have the other transports. And look at the destroyers off yonder. They are moving faster, too. I wonder if any submarine signs have been seen."

There could be no doubt that the fleet was moving faster.

"I take it," Prescott guessed, "that we've reached the part of the ocean, where greater speed is considered much more healthful."

"The leading transport is signaling, and so are the destroyers in the lead," Greg announced, peering ahead.

In their path, and coming nearer four columns of dense smoke could be observed ascending as though coming up out of the water.

"More destroyers, or some cruisers, coming out to meet us," Dick conjectured. "As yet they're too far away to be seen from this deck. Yes, I must be right. Look at the watch officers on the bridge. They are using their marine glasses and looking forward."

"More craft coming to help us?" Greg called up, after having walked nearly under the bridge end on the port side.

"Yes, sir," replied one of the watch officers. "Four American destroyers coming up to strengthen the escort."

Then he named the oncoming craft, whereat Dick Prescott started with pleasure.

"The first two are the craft commanded by Darry and Danny Grin," Dick murmured to his chum.

"That's right," Greg nodded. "I wonder if they know we're here."

"Probably not. And they wouldn't recognize us, even if they saw us at a distance. The uniform tends to make all men look alike at a very little distance. It will seem tough, though, to be so near Darry and Danny Grin and not have even a wave of the hand from them."

"What part of the ocean are we in?" Greg called up to the obliging bridge officer.

"On the surface, sir," came the dry reply. "On the surface——just where, in latitude and longitude?" Holmes insisted.

But the ship's officer smiled and shook his head.

"I'm not permitted to tell that, sir. Wish I could."

Going at the speed now employed the transport fleet and the oncoming destroyers were not long in getting to close quarters.

Dick named the two destroyers commanded by Lieutenant-Commander Dave Darrin and Lieutenant-Commander Dan Dalzell and asked the bridge officer if he could point them out. That the man above was able and very glad to do.

"We'll keep our eyes open in the hope of being close enough to signal Darry and Danny Grin," Captain Holmes suggested.

"We——" Dick began, but he stopped right there, for of a sudden three of the destroyers let go with their three-inch guns with a great deal of energy.

Two periscopes had been sighted off to northward. After a few rounds had been served from the destroyers' guns the firing ceased, for half a dozen of the escort craft had gone racing northward and there was danger of hitting them.

Not that any periscopes were now visible, however, for these had been instantly withdrawn under the surface. The destroyers, however, went alertly in search of their enemy prey, even to dropping a few depth bombs on the chance of destroying the enemy sub-sea craft.

"A good warning, at least," commented Captain Prescott. "We don't feel quite as foolish, now, in our life belts."

Everlastingly and splendidly alert the naval craft had chased off the sea wolves ere the latter had had time to bare their teeth!

Still more the speed was increased. An hour passed in which there was no alarm. Then the enlisted men, forward, filed below decks to have their early noon meal. The first lieutenants of each company went below, too, to inspect the food served to their men.

Half an hour later the Ninety-ninth's officers descended to their own mess in the cabin dining-room.

"This trip through the danger zone isn't as exciting as I had supposed and expected it would be," announced Major Wells.

"Yet, sir, one attempt was made against us this forenoon," said Dick.

"True, but the destroyers showed how promptly the attackers could be driven off," the major argued.

"Yet suppose the destroyers had been half a minute longer in sighting the tell-tale periscopes?" Prescott suggested.

"But they weren't tardy, and it wouldn't be like the Navy to be slow," rejoined Major Wells. "I still contend that there is nothing very exciting in passing through the danger zone on a troopship."

"And I hope, sir," Greg put in, "that nothing will happen to change your mind about the danger. For my part, I have been eating in momentary expectation of feeling a big smash against the side of the ship."

"What is happening now?" demanded Lieutenant Noll Terry, half-rising from his chair.

All could feel that the big ship had suddenly changed her course to a violent oblique movement to starboard. Yet, as no alarm had been sounded no officer cared to rise and hurry to deck. It might make him look timid or nervous.

"There we go again, in the opposite direction. We're zig-zagging. What do you make of that, Captain?" Lieutenant Terry asked.

"The enemy craft must be around and sending torpedoes our way," Dick guessed, dropping a lump of sugar in his coffee and stirring it slowly.

"In a merry throng like this the suspicion that you're being dogged by a hostile submarine doesn't strike one as very terrifying, does it?" Greg inquired as he took a piece of cake from the plate held out to him.

At this moment the adjutant, Captain Craig, who had been eating with Colonel Cleaves in the latter's quarters above, entered the dining-room briskly, stepping to a nearby table and rapping for attention.

"Gentlemen," he announced, "the sea appears to be infested, at this point, with unseen enemy craft. Ours, among other transports, has narrowly dodged two torpedoes. It is quite within the limits of possibility that we may be struck at any moment. The commanding officer therefore requests me to ask that company officers, especially second lieutenants, finish their meal as quickly as possible and station themselves near their men. This is not to be done hurriedly, or with any sign of excitement, but merely in order that, if we should be struck, discipline may be preserved effectively."

There was no excitement. Second lieutenants finished the morsels on which they were engaged, some of them washing down the food with a final gulp of coffee. Then, without undue haste, they left the dining-room by twos or threes.

Adjutant Craig watched them with nods of satisfaction.

"That was the right way for them to leave," he told Dick. "We do not want to throw any extra excitement in among the enlisted men, but we want them to feel that their officers are standing by, and that, at need, there will be disciplined rescue work."

Soon after the last of the platoon leaders had vanished the captains and first lieutenants made their way to the decks above.

Contrary to German reports that American soldiers are kept mostly between decks while transports are in the danger zone, the decks fore and aft were crowded with men of the Ninety-ninth. Those who stood nearest to the rails felt that they had the best vantage points from which to see what was going on. It was with eager interest, not fear, that the soldiers took in all that was visible of the fleet's progress and the work of the destroyers to protect the troopships from disaster.

From northward and slightly ahead of the course of the troopship of the Ninety-ninth a swift destroyer could be seen darting over the waves. As she came closer it seemed to the Army beholders that she traveled with the speed of an express train.

"Worth watching, and every officer and man visible on her looks and acts like a piece of the machinery," commented Major Wells, passing Prescott an extended field glass. "Want to take a look at her?"

"Why, I'd know that tall officer on her bridge anywhere in the world if I had as good a view of him as I have now," uttered Dick delightedly.

"Old Darry?" inquired Greg Holmes.

"No one else. Take a look at him. Next to the last officer on the port side of the bridge."

The instant that the glass gave him a sight of the familiar face Captain Holmes uttered a whoop.

"Darry himself, and sure enough!" Greg exclaimed. "Wonder what he's heading in so close for?"

"He knows what he's doing," Prescott returned. "Don't worry about that."

"I don't," Greg retorted cheerfully. With a rounding sweep the destroyer commanded by Dave Darrin turned out of the way of the troopship, then came up close, on the same course, scooting by.

"Good old Darry!" Prescott yelled through a megaphone that Greg thrust into his unoccupied hand.

For a wonder Dave heard, just as the destroyer darted in at her closest point to the transport.

For just an instant Darrin turned to wave his hand. Then, between both hands, placed over his mouth, he shouted:

"Hullo, Dick! 'Lo, Greg!"

Dave waved his hand, then turned to give an order to his watch officer. A brief greeting, but it meant a world to the three chums who had had a part in it.

"Now, if Danny Grin's craft would only come in that close!" sighed Greg happily.

But it didn't. Once in a while Prescott and Holmes could make out the craft commanded by Dan Dalzell, but it didn't come in close enough for a hail.

Bang! sounded a destroyer's gun, far ahead.

Bang! came as if in answer from the bowgun of the leading transport.

"There are the Huns, and here is the scrap coming!" yelled a corporal perched up in the bow of the ship.

Bang! Bang!

"Hurrah! Hurrah!" Cheers went up in such volume as to be deafening.

"Tell the men to stop that cheering," shouted Major Wells, in order to make Dick and Greg hear him. "And tell them that no more men are to crowd the rail on either side. No noise, and nothing to make the ship list!"

Going down three steps at a time, Dick and Greg descended the companionway forward of the pilot house.

"No cheering!" shouted Prescott, pushing his way through the throng. "Quiet!"

With Dick moving through the masses of soldiers on the port side of the deck, and Greg performing a similar office on the starboard side, quiet was soon restored. Then Captain Prescott's voice was heard announcing:

"You men must remain quiet, or how can the ship's officers make their orders heard? Remember, not a cheer after this. And no more men are to crowd to the rails."

"It's a pity that the rest of us cannot see what is going on!" half-grumbled a soldier, so close that Prescott heard him.

"I know just how you feel about that," the young captain admitted, wheeling and regarding the soldier. "But this is war, not sport. Absolute, uncomplaining discipline is the surest means of bringing this ship and its human cargo through safely."

Another captain and Lieutenants Terry and Overton had joined the first two officers on the deck, and order was maintained without a flaw.

Bang! bang! bang! bang!

"This sounds like a full-fledged naval battle!" Greg Holmes called to his chum, his eyes dancing.

"And we cannot see a bit of it!" sighed a soldier complainingly.

"You're in a position to see as much of it as I'm seeing, my man," Prescott retorted, with an indulgent smile. "You and I are both obeying orders instead of pleasing ourselves."

Bang! bang!

Watching some of the officers at the rail on the deck above, Captain Prescott was able to discover that the fight was being brought close to his own ship.

Then there came another sign. From up forward the port bow gun of the troopship turned itself loose with a sharp report.

"Did you note how that gun's muzzle is depressed?" Greg asked Dick, in a low voice.

"I did," Dick answered with a nod.

Bang! The port gun had been turned loose again. Up on the saloon deck the officers at the port rail were waving their campaign hats as though what they saw filled them with liveliest interest.

"I'd like to be up there!" murmured Greg in his chum's ear.

"And I'm glad I'm down here," Prescott retorted. "It shows our men that captains of the regiment are shut out from the view as much as they are. I'd like to see what is going on, but so would I like to have all these men who cannot be near the rails see what is happening."

Bang! went the starboard bow gun of the transport, her nose pointing straight ahead.

"Only one thing is plain to me," Holmes declared. "We're in the midst of a pack of the sea wolves, and they're doing their best to hit us with torpedoes!"

CHAPTER XII

Boom! It was a dull sound, off to port. Then even the men who stood in the middle of the spar deck were able to see the top of a broad column of water that rose out of the ocean.

Major Wells so far forgot himself as to give vent to a yell of joy, then suddenly clapped a restraining hand over his own mouth.

"Sorry you men couldn't have seen that," the major called, leaning over the rail above and addressing the men on the spar deck. "A destroyer let go a depth charge, which exploded under water and threw up a geyser that would make hot water feel tired."

"Look at that now, Major," urged Captain Cartwright, pulling at his superior's sleeve. Major Wells walked to the side rail, looked out over the water, and had all he could do to keep back another yell of glee.

"There's something out there that's worth seeing, men, and it's visible," the major called down. "A great blot of oil on the water, and it's spreading. That shows that a submarine was knocked to flinders by that depth charge!"

In spite of orders a low, surging cheer started.

"Shade off on that noise, men!" Dick ordered briskly, holding up his hand and moving again through the crowd. "Remember that we cannot have any racket except what the guns make."

A few more guns were fired, and the racket died down.

"The show's over!" shouted Major Wells. "Evidently we got out of that meeting with less damage than the enemy sustained. We lost no craft, while Fritz has one pirate boat less. Our destroyers of the escort are now moving along straight courses once more."

On the saloon deck many of the officers turned and stepped inside. That set the fashion, for hundreds of enlisted men left their own decks and went below, either to sleep, read or write letters.

Then, a minute later, Major Wells once more appeared at the rail forward, calling down:

"For the benefit of those who like exact statistics I will say that the commanding officer has just received a signaled message to the effect that the

71

navies of two countries got an enemy submarine apiece. You may omit the cheers!"

Those who remained on deck saw, a couple of hours later, several specks off on the water which, they were told, were British and American patrol boats out to give aid to victims of submarine sinkings.

Then night came on, dark, hazy, a bit chilling, so that officers and men alike were glad enough to seek their berths and get in under olive drab blankets.

"The haze and mist will hinder submarines anyway, so the weather is in our favor," was the word passed around.

Save for the guard, and those on other active duty, the passengers on the troopship slept soundly. They might be sunk in the night, but American fighting men do not always dwell on danger.

When first call sounded in the morning the men rubbed their eyes, then realized that the ship was proceeding at very slow speed.

"Get up, you lubbers!" called a man going down to one of the berth decks. "Do you realize that the ship is at the entrance of a French harbor?"

France?

Then a cheer went up that no officer could have stopped until it had spent its first force.

At last! France! "Over there!"

Never had men dressed faster. How the soldiers piled up the companionways! Yet a few bethought themselves to kick their now discarded life belts with a show of resentment and contempt.

However, the first glimpses had from the decks were bound to be disappointing. It was just after daylight. The mist of the night had thickened instead of vanishing. Here and there patchy bits of land could be seen through the haze, but for the most part France was invisible behind a curtain of early winter fog.

One at a time, under the guidance of local pilots, transports moved slowly into the harbor, moved slowly some more, then docked.

Here at last, made fast to a French pier constructed by American engineer troops! But where were the cheering crowds of French? Absent, for two reasons. The French had already seen many regiments of American troops arrive in former months, and the novelty of such a sight had worn off. Besides, most of the French who lived in this same port were now just about quitting their own beds.

"Who'll be first ashore from this regiment?" demanded a laughing soldier as he witnessed the work of bringing the first gangway aboard from the pier.

"The guard!" tersely replied Captain Cartwright, as he appeared with a sergeant and a detachment from the guard. As soon as the gangway had been made fast sentries were thrown out, two of them being stationed at the foot of the gangway itself.

Then came a call the soldier never ignores. The buglers sounded the first mess-call of the day.

After the meal came inspection, after which, a company at a time, the men were sent over the side to the pier. A short distance up a street the men were halted, forming in two ranks at the side of the street. The reasons for all that followed were not clear to the newer men in the ranks.

While the men had been eating between decks the officers of the regiment had gone to their last ship's meal in the dining saloon. Before the meal was half over the adjutant had entered to call out:

"At the conclusion of the meal Major Wells, Captains Prescott and Holmes and First Lieutenant Terry will report at my office for instructions from the colonel."

"That's more interesting than clear," declared Greg, as soon as he had swallowed the food in his mouth. "I wonder why we four are wanted? What have we been doing and why are we the goats?"

"Probably," smiled Dick, "it is something to do with either praise or promotion—-the two things that come most regularly to a soldier, you know."

Captain Holmes's curiosity reached such a high point that he would have bolted his food in order to get more quickly to the adjutant's office, but he noted that the battalion commander was not hurrying at all.

"Confound Wells!" the irrepressible Greg whispered to his chum. "I believe he knows what it's all about, and he knows that we cannot report before he's ready to do the same, so he's tormenting us by taking twice his usual amount of time to finish breakfast!"

"Keep cool," Dick returned dryly.

At last Major Wells finished his meal. He waited until he saw that the other three officers concerned with him in the orders had done the same. Then he inquired:

"Are you ready, gentlemen?"

Rising, Major Wells led the way above. When they entered the adjutant's office they found Colonel Cleaves standing there, chatting with a French major and two captains. Colonel Cleaves introduced his own officers, then added:

"Gentlemen, it is intended that as many as possible of the officers of this regiment shall go to the fighting front and spend some time there studying the actual war conditions. You four have been chosen for the first detail. Captain Ribaut is going to take you there. He will act as your guide and your mentor for the length of your visit to the front trenches."

Even the steady, unexcitable Major Wells showed his delight very plainly. To a soldier this was unexpected good luck, to start immediately, with the surety of finding himself speedily in the thick of things in the greatest war in the world's history!

"I have informed Captain Ribaut," Colonel Cleaves continued, "that you will be ready to leave the ship in an hour."

CHAPTER XIII

OFF TO SEE FRITZ IN HIS WILD STATE

By the time that Dick and his brother officers left the ship in the wake of Captain Ribaut, the infantrymen massed along the nearby street had been gladdened by the sight of a few score of French women and children who came to the water front to look on.

Half of the regiment was now ashore and the rest were going over the side slowly.

At the head of the pier Captain Cartwright saluted Major Wells and Captain Ribaut, and found chance to say to Prescott in a low tone:

"You're always one of the lucky ones! How do you manage it?"

"I don't know that there is any system possible in inviting luck," Dick smiled.

"You're going right up to the actual front. You'll see Fritz in his wild state. I envy you!"

"Your turn will come, Cartwright."

"It can't come too soon then. For to-day, and the next few days, I can't see anything ahead of me but drudgery."

Ever since that quarrel at Camp Berry, Cartwright had kept mostly away from Prescott and Holmes. Dick, who knew the captain for an indolent chap, didn't know whether, in other respects, he liked him. To most of the officers of the Ninety-ninth Cartwright appeared to be more unfortunate than worthless.

"Gentlemen," said Captain Ribaut, when they had passed the head of the pier, "I think that I can obtain a car if you wish it. What is your pleasure?"

"Thank you, but we've been on shipboard for so many days that we'll enjoy the chance to stretch our legs," replied Major Wells. "A walk of a few miles would do us a lot of good this morning."

"It is not that far," replied the French captain, who spoke excellent English. "The distance is, I should say, about two kilometers."

As that meant a little more than a mile the party walked off briskly.

"Why, this doesn't look really like a French town," declared Major Wells.

"You Americans have been coming here for so many months that you have made the city American," explained Captain Ribaut. "See, even the shops display signs in English, and very few in French. It is on American money that these shops thrive. Here comes one of our own poilus, a sight you will not see many times in this American town on French soil."

Poilus is a French word meaning "shaggy," and is commonly applied to the French enlisted man. As this French soldier drew close he brought up his hand in smart salute to his own officer and the Americans. Greg turned to look back, but the French soldier was no longer looking their way.

Up the street, away from where the Ninety-ninth American sentries were posted, soldiers of the American military police patrolled.

"You see how American this city has become," said Captain Ribaut. "Here French law runs only for citizens of France. Your American military authorities look after your own men."

French shopkeepers, speaking a quaint, broken English, came to their shop doors to greet the Americans, even to urge the newcomers to enter and buy, but Captain Ribaut waved all such aside with a simple gesture.

Further on they passed through a public square. By this time many French people were about, but Dick noted that they betrayed no curiosity over the appearance of newly arrived American officers. The sight had become an old story to these people who, however, bowed courteously as they passed.

Down other streets Ribaut led the way, and so they arrived at last at a railway station.

"We are about in time," remarked the Frenchman, after glancing at his wrist watch. "We shall get our seats in the train, and then we shall not wait long."

Past French guards and saluting railway employees the little party went. As the train was already made up the Frenchman led them to a first-class coach, a train guard throwing open the door. They entered and seated themselves.

"You will see that none others are shown into this compartment," said Captain Ribaut to the guard in French. The door was closed.

"After we leave the station there will be something to see," explained their guide. "Yet France is not very attractive in such weather. Up at the front, though, there is nothing at all of France left. There is nothing but bare ground, full of shell-holes. The whole face of nature has been denuded and blackened by the atrocious enemy."

When the train had been under way a couple of minutes Captain Ribaut leaned forward.

"Look over there," he said, "and you will see where your regiment will he housed for the next two or three days. After that the regiment will entrain and will go to one of the regular training camps, where you will find it on your return from the front."

His American hearers looked out on a large village of unpainted pine barracks buildings.

"That is a rest camp for troops when first they come from the transport," explained Captain Ribaut. "Even the barracks are American, built in sections in your country, then shipped over here and set up. The village you are passing will shelter two regiments of American infantry."

Before long the Americans found themselves much more interested in the French officer's conversation than in the glimpses of his country that were obtainable. Captain Ribaut had served from the beginning of the war and was familiar with every trick of fighting practiced at the front. He had a wealth of information to give them——so much, in fact, that before long Dick Prescott began to jot down information in a notebook.

Toward the end of the forenoon a soldier came aboard at one station with an outfit of dishes on two long trays. He was followed by two others bearing food and coffee. These were set out and the soldiers departed, the travelers falling to with a relish. At a station beyond, the dishes were removed by other soldiers. Then the train rolled slowly on its way.

"There is much in our travel facilities that I shall have to beg you to excuse," said Captain Ribaut rather wistfully. "France is not what it was, not even in the matter of its railways."

"France is not what she was," retorted Major Wells quickly, "because, glorious as she, was, she has gone up infinitely higher in the human scale. Could any other country in the world have stood the ravages of war so long and still live and contain so brave and resolute a people? Never mind your railways, Captain. It is the people, not the railways, who make a country. Your French people compel our constant and most willing admiration."

At another railway station, as the train halted, and the guard opened the door briefly, a low, sullen rumbling could be heard.

"Do you have thunderstorms at this time of the year, Captain?" asked Lieutenant Terry.

"Ah, but yes," replied the Frenchman. "It is a German thunderstorm that you hear in the distance——artillery."

"I feel like a fool!" exclaimed Noll Terry flushing. "Of course

I should have recognized the sound of distant cannon-fire."

"Don't feel badly about it, Mr. Terry," said Major Wells. "In all your career in the American Army you have never heard as much cannon-fire as you can hear in a single hour on the battle-front in France."

At the next station the rumbling was much louder. French soldiers were becoming more numerous. At times an entire French regiment could be seen marching along a road.

"At the next station," announced Captain Ribaut, "we shall find ourselves at the end of our rail journey. We are nearing the front. If you are interested, gentlemen, there goes one of our French airplane squadrons on its way to the front."

Instantly all four Americans were craning their necks at the windows. High in the air, the French aircraft in flight looked as graceful as swallows on the wing.

"They are battleplanes," explained Captain Ribaut further. "Some of the Hun flyers are almost sure of a tumble this afternoon."

When the American party alighted at the last station on the line, and looked back, they beheld long trains of freight cars coming slowly along. The train from which they had descended was hauled out and quickly shunted out of the way on a siding. The freight trains pulled in, going to various sidings before huge warehouses in which the food and fighting supplies were stored until wanted closer to the front. It was a scene of deafening noise and what looked like indescribable confusion. Yet everything moved according to a plan.

"Let us come where we can hear our own voices!" shouted Captain Ribaut in the major's ear, and led the way. Behind the station they found a limousine car awaiting them. As there were seats for five inside, the travelers soon found themselves vastly more comfortable than they had been on the train.

"We will drive slowly," said Captain Ribaut, after he had given his orders to a soldier chauffeur, "for one does not usually go into the trenches until after dark. There will be plenty to see on the way, and enough to talk about."

At one point Captain Ribaut directed the soldier-driver to turn the machine into a field. Here the Americans alighted to see seemingly endless streams of French "camions" go by. These are heavy motor trucks that carry supplies to the front.

"And here come some vehicles from the front that tell their own story," spoke Captain Ribaut rather sadly.

In another moment the first of a string of at least half a hundred small cars went by at rapid speed toward the rear. Each car bore the device of the Red Cross.

"There has been disagreeable work, and our wounded are going back," explained Captain Ribaut. "But my friends," he cried suddenly, "I congratulate you on what you are privileged to see. These are not our French ambulances, but some of your own cars, given to France, and young men from America are driving them."

That these were American ambulance sections in French service there could be no doubt, for as the drivers caught sight of the American uniforms they offered informal salutes in high glee. It was reserved for one gleeful young American, however, to call out, as his ambulance whizzed by:

"Hullo, buddies! Welcome to our city!"

"If that young man were in the American Army I would feel obliged to try to have him stopped," said Major Wells good-humoredly. "That was not the real American form of salutation to officers, but I know the youngster felt genuinely glad to see us so close to the front."

"They are a happy lot, perhaps sometimes a trifle too merry," said Captain Ribaut half-apologetically. "But they are splendid, these young Americans of yours who drive ambulances for us. They never know the meaning of fear, and after a great battle they are devotion itself to duty. They will drive as long as they can sit and hold the wheel. There would have been many more aching hearts in France to-day had it not been for the fine young Americans who came over here with American cars to help us look after our wounded!"

Presently the party entered the car again. Every mile that they covered took them closer to the Inferno of shell-fire. More ambulance cars whizzed by.

Then the visitors' car drew up before an unpretentious looking house just off the main road.

"If you will come inside," invited Captain Ribaut, "I know that our general of division will be delighted to meet you."

CHAPTER XIV

THE THRILL OF THE FIRE TRENCH

Passing the two sentries at the front door the officers found themselves in a small ante-room.

Excusing himself, Captain Ribaut left the Americans briefly, but was speedily back.

"General Bazain is most eager to meet you, and has the leisure at this moment," the Frenchman announced.

He led his guests through the adjoining room, where half a dozen younger French officers rose hastily, standing at salute. Then on into a third room, just over the sill of which Captain Ribaut halted, bringing his heels quickly together as he called out:

"General Bazain, I have the honor to present to you four American officers, Major——-"

And so on, through the list of names. The French divisional commander bowed courteously four separate times, taking each American officer by the hand with both his own, and finding something wholly courteous to say. He spoke in French, a tongue that only Major Wells and Captain Prescott understood well.

"My division is greatly honored, *Messieurs les Officers*," General Bazain continued when he had seen to the seating of his callers and had resumed his own chair behind a desk on which were spread many maps and documents.

"You have been having a smart fight this afternoon, sir?" inquired Major Wells.

"Ah, yes, for some reason, the Huns have been trying to break through my division this afternoon, but they have not yet succeeded, nor will they," General Bazain added, his eyes flashing grimly.

He was a little man, short and thin, his hair well sprinkled with gray. He looked like one whom more than three years of war had borne down with cares, yet his eyes were bright and his shoulders squared splendidly whenever he stood.

"Here is a map of the divisional front, gentlemen, if you care to draw your chairs closer and look it over," proposed the general. "This shows not only our lines, but as much as we know of the enemy lines facing us. And I believe," he added, with another flash of pride, "that we know all there is to know of their lines for a kilometer back, except whatever may have been added since dark yesterday. We———"

He was interrupted by an explosion that shook the house. It sounded over their heads on the floor above.

"We have excellent air service at this point," General Bazain went on, his attention not wavering from the map. "And at this point, as you will see, we have five lines of trenches, one behind another, instead of three. It would take the Hun an uncommonly long time to drive my brave fellows back out of our five lines of trenches."

There followed a rapid description of the work of the division on that sector during the last four months. The two present first lines of trench had been taken from the Germans. Plans were now under way to stage a series of assaults which, it was hoped, would drive the Huns out of their three present first lines of trench and add them to the French system.

An officer wearing the emblem of the French medical service opened the door and glanced in.

"My general, you were not hurt by that bomb?" he cried anxiously.

"I had forgotten it," replied the French divisional commander. "What was it?"

"A Hun airman dropped a bomb on the roof. It blew a hole in the roof and worked some damage in your bedroom overhead."

"It does not matter," said General Bazain simply.

Bang! bang! smashed overhead.

"It must be the same rascal, returning in his flight!" cried the medical officer, darting out into the yard to look up at the sky. A moment later anti-aircraft guns began to bark. Two minutes after the medical officer again looked into the room.

"We are fortunate to-day, my general!" cried the doctor. "That scoundrel will not bother you again. One of our shots wrecked his plane and brought the Hun down—-dead."

Evidently, however, that airman of the enemy had given the location and range of division headquarters, for now a shell from a German battery struck and exploded in the yard outside, killing a sentry and wounding two orderlies. A second and a third shell followed. A fourth shell tore away the corner of the house without injuring any one.

"Your orders, my general, in case our observers can locate the Hun battery?" asked a staff officer, coming in from the next room and resting a hand on a telephone instrument.

"If the enemy battery can be located," replied General Bazain, "let it be destroyed."

Rapidly the staff officer sent his message to the artillery post of command.

"But surely you will go to a shelter?" asked the staff officer, laying down the instrument when he had finished.

"It will be inconvenient," sighed the division commander. "The light here is much better."

Yet General Bazain permitted himself to be persuaded to remove from this now highly dangerous spot. As he and his staff, accompanied by the visitors, stepped outside another shell exploded close at hand, fortunately without doing harm.

Descending to the cellar of a wrecked house near by, in the wake of their hosts, the Americans found the entrance to steps, cut in the earth, leading to a secure shelter on a level much below that of the cellar. Here were two rooms underground, both equipped with desks, lights, chairs, telephones and all that was needed for communicating with the ranking officers of the division at their posts in the trenches.

"It is stupid to have to work under candlelight in the daytime," sighed the division commander. "However, Major Wells, as I was explaining to you ———."

Here recourse was again had to the maps, which the officers of the staff had brought along.

Before dark supper was served at division headquarters in this dug-out reached through the cellar of a ruined house.

"If it were not that I expect an attack tonight, and must be at my post, it would give me delight to go with you and show you our trenches," said the division commander at parting.

Private Berger had been summoned to lead the party through the intricate system of communication trenches to the front. Berger, who was a short, squat fellow with a sallow face and uneasy black eyes, took his seat beside the soldier chauffeur.

For only a little more than a mile the Americans proceeded in the car, which then halted, and all hands stepped out into the dark night.

"From here on we must walk," announced Captain Ribaut. "Berger, be sure that you take us by the most direct route. Do not take us into the Hun trenches to-night."

"I know the way excellently, my captain," Berger replied briefly.

For some distance they walked over open country, made dangerous, however, by the presence of gaping shell-holes. Runners, soldiers and others passed them going to or from the trenches. The artillery duel, save for an occasional stray shot, had ceased on both sides.

"The road is steeper here," said Berger, halting after he had led his party half a mile through the darkness. "We now go up hill."

It was harder climbing, going up that incline. A quarter of a mile of this, and Lieutenant Terry suddenly found himself following the guide through a cut in between two walls of dirt higher than his head.

"We are in the communication trenches," said Berger in French. Noll gathered the meaning of the remark.

At every few yards there was a twist or a turn in the trench. At times they came to points where two trenches crossed each other. Had it been left to the Americans to find their own way they would have been hopelessly confused in this network and maze of intersecting ditches. Berger, however, proceeded with the certainty of one long familiar with the locality.

"Here is one of our defence trenches," said Captain Ribaut, halting at last and calling softly to Berger to stop. "This is our fifth line trench, formerly our third line. We have no men here, you will note, nor in the next line. In case of a heavy general attack men would be rushed up from the rear to occupy these two lines of trenches. We will proceed, Berger."

They were soon at the fourth line trench. At the third line trench they found sentries of the reserves on duty.

"The rest of the reserves are sleeping," Ribaut explained. "You will see their dug-out entrances as we pass along this trench, for I am taking you to the quarters of the battalion commander."

It was necessary to proceed along this third line trench for nearly a quarter of a mile before they came to a dug-out entrance before which a sentry and two runners crouched on the ground.

"Captain Ribaut and American officers present their compliments, and would see Major Ferrus," explained Ribaut.

A runner entered the underground shelter, speedily returning and signing to the visitors to descend the steps. Dick and his friends found themselves in an underground room of about eight by twelve. Around the walls were several bunks. At a table, which held a telephone instrument, sat Major Ferrus and two junior officers.

"It is quiet here, after the Hun assault of this afternoon," explained the French major when the Americans had been presented. "Captain Ribaut, you are taking our American comrades to the front line?"

"That is my instruction, Major."

"It is well, and I think you will find it quiet enough to-night for a study of the Hun line. Still one can never say."

A brief conversation, and the visitors returned to the outer air, where Private Berger awaited them. At the second line trench, which held the supporting troops for the first line, Ribaut took them to the captain of French infantry in command at that point.

"I will send Lieutenant De Verne with you," said the captain, and passed the word for that officer.

"Show our American comrades everything that can possibly interest them," was the captain's order.

"I shall do my best, my captain," replied the lieutenant. "But I do not know. The Huns are as quiet, to-night, as though they had tired themselves to death this afternoon."

Turning to Private Berger, Lieutenant De Verne added:

"You may find your way into one of the dugouts if you like, as you will hardly be needed for hours."

"But my orders, my lieutenant, were to remain with the American party," protested Private Berger mildly.

"Oh, very well, then," replied De Verne carelessly.

This time, instead of leading the way, Private Berger brought up the rear.

"You will do well to talk in low tones," the French lieutenant cautioned them in whispers, "for, when we enter the front line trench we shall be only about a quarter of a kilometer from the Huns' first line trench."

With that they started forward. A short stroll through a communication trench brought them to the first line ditch. As the ground was wet here duck-boards had been laid to walk on. The parapet was piled high with bags of sand through which loop-holes had been cunningly contrived for the French sentries who must watch through the night for signs of Hun activity. Over the rear wall of the trench was another built-up wall of sand-bags. This parados, as it was called, is intended to give protection against shrapnel, which often burst just after passing over a trench. Thus the parados prevents a back-fire of the bullets carried in the shrapnel shell, which otherwise might strike the trench's defenders.

"You may stand up here on the fire platform, if you wish," whispered Lieutenant De Verne to Dick in English. "If you do not think it too foolish to expose yourself, you will be able to look over the top of the parapet. First of all you will see our lines of barbed wire fencing and entanglements. Beyond the wire you will see open ground, much torn by shell-holes. Further still you will see the wire defenses of the German first trench, and then the parapet that screens the enemy from your gaze."

Hardly had the French lieutenant finished when Dick was up and peering with all his might and curiosity. Hardly an instant later the bark of a field-gun was heard to the northward. A whining thing whizzed through the air.

Then, into the trench in which the party stood something thudded, with, at the same instant, a sharp report, a bright flash, and the air was full of flying metal!

CHAPTER XV

If there was a disgusted person present it was Captain Greg Holmes. That angry young man spat out a mouthful of dirt, and then tried to rid himself of more.

Major Wells felt more like standing on his head. A fragment of shell had torn away the top of his tunic in back, without scratching his skin, and at the same time had thrown a shower of sand down inside his O.D. woolen shirt. Terry had been knocked over by the concussion, but had sustained no wound and was quickly on his feet, unhurt.

As for Prescott, he had turned, for an astounded second, then, much disturbed over what he believed to have been his fault, he had stepped down from the fire step.

Captain Ribaut and Lieutenant De Verne, neither of whom had been touched, looked on and smiled.

As Prescott stepped down to the duck-boards he saw Private Berger come back into the trench from the adjoining traverse, the latter a jog in the trench line intended to prevent the enemy from raking any great length of trench during an attack.

"I hadn't an idea that just raising my head over the parapet would bring cannon fire so promptly," Dick murmured to Ribaut.

"Nor did that act of yours bring cannon fire," rejoined Captain Ribaut.

"Then what did?"

"It must have been that it just happened," replied the Frenchman.

Private Berger stood leaning with his right hand on top of the sand-bag parapet.

"Shall I get back on the fire step for another look?" Dick inquired.

"Why not?" inquired Captain Ribaut, shrugging his shoulders. "Why not, indeed, if there is anything you wish to see?"

Waiting for no more Dick again mounted to the fire step, raising his head over the top, this time with greater caution.

"There it is again!" he cried, in a voice scarcely above a whisper, his words causing his friends astonishment.

A moment later there came another sharp report, followed by the same whining sound. This time a shell struck just behind the parados. There was an avalanche of shell fragments, but none flew into the trench, the parados preventing.

"Captain Ribaut, a word with you," Dick urged, stepping down and laying a hand on the French officer's arm. They stepped further along the trench.

"Captain," Prescott whispered earnestly, "I do not want to arouse any unfair suspicions, but I have something to tell you. When I first looked over the parapet I noticed on the ground in front three small but distinct glows. Then came the report and the shell. Private Berger had stepped into the traverse at his right. Immediately after the shell burst he came back into this trench. When I looked over the top a second time I saw the same three tiny glows of light on the ground ahead. Then came the second shell. Each time, before the shell was started this way Berger stood with his right hand resting above his head on the parapet. Each time he stepped down and into the traverse. Each time, after the shell burst, he stepped back into this trench. I may be wrong to feel any suspicions, but is it possible——-"

"Wait!" interposed Captain Ribaut quickly, and stepped into the traverse at the left. He came back with two French soldiers. These started down the trench, pouncing upon Private Berger. With them was Captain Ribaut.

"Oh, you scoundrel, Berger!" suddenly hissed the French captain. He hurled the fellow to the ground, then held up a slim object, some six inches in length.

"See!" he muttered to the others. "It is a tiny electric light, supplied by a very small special battery. The scoundrel, Berger, had it concealed up his right sleeve. Twice he rested his right hand on the parapet. He flashed the lamp thrice each time, for Captain Prescott saw it. Then the scoundrel stepped into the traverse, where he would be safe from the shell he had invoked from the enemy. We have known that there was a spy or a traitor in this regiment, but we were unable to identify him. Gentlemen, step into the traverses on either side and I will test my belief."

After the others had filed into the traverses Captain Ribaut rested his right hand on the parapet, causing the little pencil of electric light to glow three times in quick succession. Then he sprang back into the nearer traverse.

Bang! A shell landed in the vacated length of trench, tearing up the duck-boards and gouging the walls of the trench.

"Go for your corporal and tell him to send two men to take this spy to the rear," Ribaut ordered one of the soldiers who stood guarding Berger. "Captain Prescott, this regiment owes you a debt that it will never be able to repay. Berger, your hours of life will be short, but the story of your infamy will be everlasting!"

"And, Corporal," ordered Lieutenant De Verne, after Berger had been started rearward under guard, "see to it that only the most necessary sentries are posted along here for tonight. Keep the rest of your men in shelters, for the Huns may feel disposed to continue shelling this part of the line."

"Come, my American comrades," urged Captain Ribaut, "there is much more to be seen at other points along this line."

Until within an hour of daylight the French captain and lieutenant and their American pupils continued along the first line trench. Save for occasional shell fire it proved to be a rather quiet night. Leaving the front a sufficient time before dawn Major Wells and his subordinates went back to the fifth line trench. After breakfasting, they retired to bunks that had been bedded in advance of their coming, and slept until late in the afternoon.

"There is one thing I like about the French trenches," declared Greg Holmes, with enthusiasm, as soldiers entered with the beginnings of a meal.

"And what is that?" inquired Captain Ribaut eagerly.

"The smell of the coffee when it comes in," grinned Greg.

"To-day's sleep, and the meals, I have found to be of the best," said Captain Dick quietly, as he sat down to eat. "I am still more interested in the hope that to-night in the fire trenches will be more exciting than last night."

"Perhaps it will be," suggested Captain Ribaut, "for I have received word that patrols will be sent out into No Man's Land to-night, and it has been suggested to me that one American officer should go with the patrol. Which one of you shall it be?"

"I know that Captain Prescott wants to go," said Major Wells, as he noted Dick's start of pleasure. "Therefore, Captain Ribaut, suppose you send him with the patrol."

"Thank you, sir," came Dick's quick assent. "Nothing could please me more. It will make to-night a time surely worth while to me."

Before the meal had been finished the German artillerymen began the late afternoon "strafing," as a bombardment is called.

When the shell-fire had ceased Ribaut led his guests down to the front or fire trench. Lieutenant De Verne had not been with them since breakfast time in the morning.

"May I relieve one of your sentries, Captain, and take his post until there is something else for me to do?" Dick asked.

"Yes, certainly," agreed Ribaut. "I will send for the corporal, who will instruct you as the other sentries are instructed."

So Dick took the bayoneted rifle of a soldier who was much delighted at having a brief opportunity for sleep thus thrust upon him. Dick listened to the corporal's orders, then, for the next two hours stood gazing patiently out over No Man's Land. At the end of that time the sentries were changed and Dick stood down gladly enough, for his task had become somewhat dull and irksome.

Half an hour after being relieved Prescott heard a sentry challenging in low tones. Then Lieutenant De Verne came into the fire trench with a sergeant and six men.

"This is the patrol," announced the younger Frenchman. "All my men for to-night are veterans at the game. Captain Prescott, do you wish to try your hand as a bomber tonight?"

"I am more expert, Lieutenant, with an automatic pistol."

"Very good, then; you may stick to that weapon," agreed the lieutenant. "The sergeant and three men will carry their rifles; the other three men will serve as bombers. You observe that our faces and hands are blackened, as white faces betray one in No Man's Land. We will now help you to black up."

There followed some quick instructions, to all of which Dick listened attentively, for to him it was a new game.

"We have little gates cut through our own barbed wire," De Verne whispered in explanation. "Do not be in a hurry, Captain, when you leave the trench. Especially, take pains that you do not catch your clothing on any of the barbed wire as we crawl through."

A few more whispered directions. While listening Dick studied the faces of the waiting French soldiers, their bearing and their equipment. Only the sergeant remained standing; the privates disposed of themselves on the fire step for a seat. Two of them even dozed, so far were they from any feeling of excitement.

"Ready, now, Sergeant," nodded the lieutenant.

"We are ready, Lieutenant," reported the sergeant.

"Proceed."

First of all the sergeant went up over the top of the trench, crawling noiselessly to the ground beyond. After him, one at a time, went the French soldiers.

"You next, Captain, if you please," urged Lieutenant De Verne. "And do not forget that any betraying sound causes the night to be lighted with German flares and that the Huns are always ready to turn their machine guns loose."

Dick's hands were instantly on the rungs of the ladder. Up he went, cat-like. By the time that he had crawled over the parapet and had reached the first fence of tangled barbed wire be found a French soldier, prostrate on the ground, waiting, and holding open a gate that had been ingeniously cut through the mantrap. Then the soldier crawled on to the next line of wire defence, repeating the service, as also at a third line.

The last wire had now been passed. Still lying nearly flat, Captain Prescott raised his head, staring ahead into the nearly complete blackness of the night. He was in No Man's Land!

CHAPTER XVI

THE TRIP THROUGH A GERMAN TRENCH

It was the sergeant who led the way. He and his detail moved, except at special times, in a fan-shaped formation with the noncommissioned officer ahead, three men on either side of him formed lines obliquely back.

In the center, within these oblique flanks were the French lieutenant and Captain Prescott.

It was a compact formation, useful in keeping all hands together and in instant touch, yet likely to prove highly dangerous should the enemy open on them with rifle or machine-gun fire.

In the center of No Man's Land was a wide, deep shell crater, caused by the explosion at that point of one of the largest shells used by the Germans.

Crawling down between friendly and hostile lines, the sergeant made for this shell-hole. When still several feet away he held up a hand, whereupon Lieutenant De Verne gripped Prescott's leg. Leaving the others behind the noncommissioned officer moved silently forward. It was his task to make sure that an enemy party had not been first to reach the crater.

Only eyes trained to see in that darkness could make out the fact that the sergeant had held up a hand once more. This was the signal to advance. Now, as the men moved forward, the formation was not kept. Each for himself reached the crater in his own way and time. Down in this basin men could crouch without fear of being seen should the night become lighted up.

When the others had entered, Prescott, being further from the rim, signed to the French lieutenant to precede him. De Verne had just gained the hole when ——Click! Not far away something was shot up into the air; then it broke, throwing down a beam of light. Other clicks could be heard, until the land within two hundred feet of the crater became at least half as bright as daylight would have made it.

Dick Prescott was outside the crater! At the instant of hearing the first click he found himself in a shallow furrow in the dirt. To have sprung into the crater would have been to betray the presence of the party to the enemy. While German machine-gun fire could not reach the French men below him Dick knew that a shell could reach them readily enough.

So he flattened himself in the furrow, his heart beating faster than usual. There followed moments of tight suspense. Would this flattened figure be espied by any enemy observer?

Even when the flares died down Dick did not move. He knew that more flares might be sent up instantly.

A quarter of a mile down the line he could hear a machine gun rouse itself into sudden fury, though none of the missiles came his way.

"I've a chance yet," Dick thought grimly. Yet when blackness came down over the scene again he did not move. No matter what happened to himself he did not intend that harm should come to his French comrades through any act of his.

As Dick still lay there a pebble touched the dirt lightly just before his face. Raising his head a couple of inches he saw a hand, dimly outlined at the edge of the crater, beckoning.

"That means that I'm to go ahead," Dick told himself. "I'll follow instructions."

He took considerable time about it, moving an inch or two at a time. This, however, soon brought him to the edge of the basin-like depression. In going down the inside he moved a bit more rapidly, but did not rise until he found himself among the others. Then he rose to his knees in the middle of the group.

"You are wonderful!" whispered the French lieutenant, placing his lips at Prescott's ear. "You Americans must have learned your stealth from your own Indians. We are clumsy when we try to equal you in moving without noise."

One of the soldiers had taken station at the edge of the crater nearest the German line. Here, with helmet off, and showing not a fraction of an inch more of his head above ground than was necessary, this sentry watched in the dark.

Again De Verne's lips sought Dick's ear as he whispered:

"What we would like most to do is to find out what is going on in the Hun trenches. Next to that, the thing we like best is to ambush a German patrol, capture or kill the men, and get back with our prisoners."

"French patrols must often be captured, also," Dick whispered cautiously.

"But yes!" replied the French lieutenant, with a shrug of his shoulders. "It is a game of give-and-take, and all the luck cannot be ours."

Still nearer the enemy's wire defenses lay a smaller shell-hole. By creeping up beside the sentry Prescott was able to see it. He remained where he was while a soldier of the French party, holding a bomb in his right hand, crept out of the crater, moving noiselessly ahead.

Arrived at the edge of the smaller shell-hole the soldier sent back a hand signal, then crept down into concealment.

Up out of the crater started the sergeant without delay. As he passed Prescott the noncommissioned officer gripped him, pointing backward. There knelt De Verne, signaling to the American to accompany the sergeant. Side by side the pair made the smaller shell-hole, which proved of just sufficient size to screen three men.

For three or four minutes the trio crouched here, listening intently, though no sounds came from the nearby German trench.

After waiting, as he thought, long enough, the French sergeant made an expressive gesture or two before the face of the soldier with him, who, after examining his bombs, crept out and forward, toward the barbed wire defenses of the enemy.

Short though the distance was, the man was gone more than five minutes. Prescott, who at first could see the soldier as he moved, was not so sure of it later. It was strange how that sky-blue uniform of the poilu merged into the dark shades of the night.

At last the soldier came back, reporting to his sergeant, though using only the language of hand signs.

With a nudge for Prescott the sergeant crept out of the hole, Dick following. There was no thought of haste, yet at last they reached the first of the wire obstructions. Now Dick was able to guess the meaning of the soldier's recent hand signs. He had discovered that the Huns had left narrow passages through their own wires, presumably for the use of German patrols.

This time it was the sergeant who went forward first. Dick thrilled with admiration when he saw the French non-com pass the last of the barbed wire and creep up to the top of the German parapet, flattening himself and peering over and down.

Following closely Dick and the French soldier at his side saw the sergeant kick up slightly with one foot, a signal that caused the soldier to move to the top of the parapet; Prescott, therefore did the same thing.

It was his first look down into a German trench! Not that there was much to be seen. On the contrary there was nothing to be seen save the trench itself. Dick had heard that often the German first-line trenches are deserted during parts of quiet nights on the front.

A slight sense of motion caused Prescott to look around. He was in time to see the French private wriggling backward. The sergeant withdrew his head to a point below the outer edge of the parapet, seeing which the American captain followed suit.

Minutes passed before the departed soldier returned with Lieutenant De Verne and the remainder of the patrol. Only a glance did the French lieutenant take down into the trench. Next he quietly let himself down into the enemy ditch, followed by the others.

Moving softly the patrol examined that length of trench, also the traverses at either end. Still no German had been encountered.

"We will go further," announced Lieutenant De Verne. "Sergeant, you will take three men and go west until you come in contact with the enemy. Then return with your report. The rest of us will go east."

Carrying a bomb in his right hand, a pistol in his left the young French officer led the way. Just behind him was one of his own infantrymen, Prescott coming third and carrying his automatic pistol ready for instant use.

Counting the number of trench sections and traverses through which they passed Dick estimated that they moved east fully two hundred yards. In all that distance they did not encounter a German soldier.

"The Huns who sent up the flares," De Verne paused to whisper to Dick, "must have been the last of the enemy in these trenches. It made them appear to be on guard, and vigilantly so, and right after sending up the flares they withdrew to lines at the rear. It is, I suspect, an old trick of theirs when they wish to leave the front to rest or feed. I shall so report it."

At last the lieutenant halted his men. He had penetrated as far as he deemed necessary.

"We will go back and pick up the sergeant," he said. "But first I shall send a man down one of the communication trenches to learn if the enemy are numerous in the second-line trenches."

"How long will that take?" Dick whispered.

"At least ten minutes."

"Then may I try to penetrate a little further east along this line?"

"Why not?"

"I will try to be back soon," Dick promised. Even in the darkness these Allied officers exchanged salutes smartly. Then, gripping his automatic tightly, and realizing that he was now "on his own," as the British Tommies put it, he disappeared into the nearest traverse.

Prescott did not hurry. He had nothing to expect from his own little prowl, and his purpose in going alone had been to develop his knowledge of this new kind of soldier's work.

Sixty or seventy yards Dick had progressed when, in a traverse, he thought he heard low voices ahead.

"The enemy, if any one!" he thought, with a start, halting quickly. Straining his ears, he listened. Undoubtedly there were voices somewhere ahead, though he could distinguish no word that was spoken.

"As I haven't seen an enemy yet, I'm going to do so if I can," the young captain instantly resolved.

Stepping to the end of the traverse, he peered around the jog. That next length of trench appeared to be deserted, yet certainly the voices sounded nearer.

"I've got to have that look!" Dick told himself, exulting in the chance.

Softly he strode forward, then halted all in a flash. And no wonder! For he found himself standing close to the entrance to a frontline dug-out that sloped down into the earth. And the voices came from this dug-out.

Inside, as Dick peered down, he made out two figures. Yet he pinched himself with his unoccupied hand, so certain did it seem that he must be dreaming.

Of the pair below, while the older man wore the uniform of a German colonel of infantry, the younger man wore the garb of a French sub-lieutenant of the same arm. What could this infernal mystery mean?

CHAPTER XVII

DICK PRESCOTT'S PRIZE CATCH

It was the older man, he of the German uniform who now spoke.

"So Berger was really caught in the act of signaling us?"

"Yes, excellenz (Your excellency)," replied the younger man.

"And he is to be shot for treason?"

"It is so, Excellenz!"

The language used by both was German, but Dick followed every word easily.

"Too bad! And our commander will regret the loss of Berger much," sighed the German colonel, "for Berger has served us long and usefully. Strange that he should be caught, when he has so long and safely used that electric light pencil of his. I suppose Berger grew careless."

"It was an American officer who caught him at it and denounced him," said the younger man.

"Ah, well! At least we have you still in that regiment, and you are more cautious. You will not be caught."

"Not alive, at any rate, Excellenz," the younger man assured the enemy colonel.

"Wrong, there!" spoke a low, firm voice.

Both men started violently, with good excuse, for before them stood Captain Dick Prescott, a cocked automatic pistol held out to cover both.

"You will both put your hands up!" Dick ordered them sharply, in German. "You will be shot at the first sign of resistance, or even reluctance. This trench is no longer German!"

Dully both men raised their hands. Quietly as Prescott spoke there was that in his tone, as in his eye, which assured them that their lives would not outlast their obedience.

"You will pass up before me," Dick continued, "and neither will attempt any treachery. I assure you, gentlemen, that I shall be glad of the slightest excuse for killing you!"

It was the German colonel who came first, for he was the nearer one. There was no visible sign of his being armed, but the younger man in the sky-blue uniform carried an automatic in a holster at his belt. Dick deftly took the pistol from the holster and was now doubly armed.

"Not the lightest outcry, nor the least attempt at treachery!" Dick warned them sternly. "Face west! March!"

Though both prisoners obeyed promptly Captain Prescott was not simple enough to imagine that they had no plan or hope of rescue or escape. In making this double arrest Dick had realized fully that he was probably throwing his life away, yet he had deemed possible success worth all the risk.

After going thirty or forty yards the older prisoner halted squarely.

"Proceed!" Dick ordered in a stern whisper, aiming one of the pistols at the defiant one's breast.

"I do not care about being killed needlessly; neither do you," said the colonel. "I can save my life, and give you some chance for yours by informing you that, at the moment you appeared in the dug-out, I pressed one foot against a signal apparatus that calls our men back to these trenches. Just now I heard them entering a trench section ahead. Others have entered behind us. Your chance, your only one, will be to climb over this parapet and do your best to reach the French lines. If you decide to do that, I give you my word that I will not allow our men to fire upon you as you withdraw."

"A German's word!" mocked Dick. "Who would accept that?"

"It is your last chance for life."

"And you are throwing away your last chance, both of you!" Dick uttered in a low voice. "Each of you is within a second of death. March!"

With an exclamation that sounded like an oath the German colonel obeyed, followed by the younger man and Prescott. Neither of the prisoners had dared risk lowering his hands.

"You are foolish——life-tired!" warned the colonel, in a hoarse whisper.

"If you speak again I'll kill you instantly," Prescott snapped back.

After that the prisoners proceeded in moody silence, until, at last, they rounded out a traverse and ran into several soldiers. But these soldiers wore the French uniform. In a word, they were Lieutenant De Verne's party.

"Prisoners!" cried De Verne, in a hoarse whisper. "Captain Prescott, you are indeed wonderful! But no, you bring only one prisoner, this German, for the other is Lieutenant Noyez. Noyez, my dear fellow, how do you happen to have your hands up?"

"Because of the idiocy of this American," hissed Noyez.

"Lieutenant De Verne, from the conversation that I overheard I learned that Noyez is a spy, and that he was reporting to his chief, this enemy colonel," Dick stated. "Now that I have brought them to you, both are naturally in your hands."

"It is a stupid lie that you, De Verne, must set straight," Noyez insisted angrily.

"Since Captain Prescott has made the charge, it must stand, of course, until you have been taken before competent authority," De Verne said coldly. "Pirot! Grugny! I turn Lieutenant Noyez over into your charge. You will give him no chance to get out of your hands. And now, we must find our way home."

Two men were sent up over the parapet, then the prisoners were ordered up and held there at the muzzles of rifles. The rest of the patrol followed.

"We will make fast time back," ordered Lieutenant De Verne, "as we know there are no enemy hereabouts in the first-line trenches."

Crossing rapidly, though softly, the patrol was challenged by a sentry in the French trench. De Verne went forward to answer and to establish the identity of his patrol. Then they were allowed to pass in by the wire defenses, and next descended to the trench. Officers and men hurriedly cleansed the black from their hands and faces.

"We will now march to Captain Cartier," said De Verne, "and he shall give us our further orders."

"You are looking for your friends, Captain?" spoke up a French soldier in the trench, in his own tongue. "Captain Ribaut has taken them west along the line."

"Thank you. If they return, you will tell them where I have gone."

By this time the German colonel was cursing volubly. He felt that he could talk, at last, without danger of being killed for his audacity. Noyez, pallid as in death, was silent, his eyes cast down.

Back to the third line of trenches De Verne led the party, then down into the dug-out of his company commander, Captain Cartier.

"A German colonel and Lieutenant Noyez, prisoners!" announced the patrol leader.

"The German colonel I can understand truly," replied the French captain. "But why Lieutenant Noyez?"

"Captain Prescott, of the American Army, arrested both and made the charges against Noyez," De Verne responded. "You will hear him now?"

As it was their first meeting Captain Cartier shook hands with Dick, who then told what he had overheard.

"Noyez, a German spy!" exclaimed Captain Cartier. "Truly, it seems incredible."

"It is worse! It is an infamous charge!" cried Noyez passionately.

"Yet our American comrade must be truthful, a man of honor," said Captain Cartier, in a bewildered tone.

"May I suggest, sir," Dick interposed, "that it will be easy to decide. If Lieutenant Noyez was in the German trenches by orders of his superiors, or with their knowledge, then that would establish a first point in his favor. But if he was there without either orders or permission, then plainly he must have gone there on treasonable business."

"That is absolutely fair!" declared Captain Cartier. "I will send at once for Noyez's captain, and we shall hear what he says."

In dejected silence Noyez awaited the arrival of Captain Gaulte, who promptly declared that he had no knowledge of any authority for his lieutenant to visit the enemy's lines. Gaulte had, in fact, supposed that Noyez was back of the lines on over-night leave, for which he had applied.

"The business looks bad!" cried Captain Cartier, with troubled face.

"Quite!" agreed Captain Gaulte more calmly.

"I must telephone for instructions," Cartier continued. "It may require a long wait. Gentlemen, you will find seats."

First Cartier called up his regimental commander and reported the matter.

"It will be passed on to division headquarters," reported Captain Cartier, turning from the telephone instrument.

By and by the telephone bell tinkled softly. Orders came over the wire that the arresting party should take the prisoners to division headquarters.

"These are your instructions, then, Lieutenant De Verne. Of course it is expected that Captain Prescott will accompany you as complaining witness."

In the darkness of the night it was a toilsome march back through the communication trenches. This time, when they were left behind, there was no limousine to pick up the members of the party.

"It is a relief to be at last where we can talk," said De Verne, in English.

"You may speak for yourself," retorted the German colonel gruffly, betraying the fact that he understood the language.

Halted four times by sentries, the party at last reached division headquarters. Outside a young staff officer awaited them.

"General Bazain has risen and dressed," stated the staff officer. "He had undertaken to snatch two hours' sleep, but this cannot be his night to sleep. The general awaits you, and you are to enter. Through to his office."

As they entered the division commander's office they found that fine old man pacing his room in evident agitation.

"And you, too, Noyez?" he called, in a tone of astounded reproach. "It was bad enough that we should find Berger a spy! But to find one of our trusted officers—-it is too much!"

"I am neither spy nor traitor, my general!" declared Noyez furiously, "and my record should remove the least suspicion from my name."

"But you were in the enemy's trenches this night, without knowledge or leave of your superiors, Lieutenant. Have you a plausible way to account for it?"

"All in good time, my general, when my head has had time to clear," promised the young sub-lieutenant.

"It is but fair that we give you time," assented General Bazain. "It can give France no joy to find one of her officers a traitor."

It was now the German's turn to be questioned. He gave his name as Pernim. As he was an ordinary prisoner of war he was led from the room to be turned over to the military prison authorities.

"And it was you, my dear Captain Prescott, who captured one spy who has since admitted his guilt. And now you bring in another whom you accuse."

"Berger has confessed, sir," Dick asked, "may I inquire if he implicated Lieutenant Noyez?"

"He did not."

"Yet, sir, from what I heard, Berger and Noyez worked together. If Berger be informed that Noyez has been captured is it not likely that Berger will then tell of this accused man's work?"

"Excellent suggestion! We shall soon know!" exclaimed General Bazain, touching a bell.

CHAPTER XVIII

A LOT MORE OF THE REAL THING

Through the orderly who answered, three staff officers were summoned. To these the general gave his orders in undertones in a corner of the room. As the three hastened out not one of them sent as much as a glance in the direction of the unhappy Noyez.

Seating himself in his chair General Bazain, after courteously excusing himself, closed his eyes as though to sleep. The arresting party and Noyez withdrew to the adjoining room.

More than an hour passed ere the three staff officers returned and hastened into the division commander's office. Fifteen minutes after that Dick and his friends, with the prisoner, were again summoned.

"It has been simpler than we thought," General Bazain announced wearily. "Berger, when questioned and informed of Noyez's arrest, confessed that Noyez was the superior spy under whom he worked."

"It is a lie, my general!" exclaimed Noyez, in a choking voice, as he strode forward, only to be seized and thrust back.

"It is the truth!" retorted General Bazain, rising and glaring at the accused man. "Berger not only confessed, but he told where, in your dug-out, Noyez, could be found the secret compartment in which you hid the book containing the key to the code you sometimes employed in sending written reports to the enemy. And here is the code book!"

General Bazain tossed the accusing little notebook on the desk.

At sight of that Noyez fell back three steps, then sank cowering into a chair, covering his eyes with his hands.

"You comprehend that further lying will avail you nothing!" the division commander went on sternly. "Lieutenant De Verne!"

"Here, sir!"

"Noyez, stand up. Lieutenant De Verne, I instruct you to remove from the uniform of Noyez the insignia of his rank and every emblem that stands for France! That done, you will next cut the buttons from Noyez's tunic!"

Standing so weakly that it looked as if he must fall, Noyez submitted to the indignity, silent save for the sobs that choked his voice.

"Call in the guard, and have the wretch removed from my sight!" General Bazain ordered. "Yet, Noyez, I will say that it seems to me incredible that any Frenchman could have been so ignoble as you have proved yourself to he."

"A Frenchman?" repeated Noyez disdainfully. "No Frenchman am I. Already I am condemned, so I no longer need even pretend that I am French. No! Though I was born in Alsace, my father's name was Bamberger. Twenty years ago he moved to Paris, to serve the German Kaiser. He fooled even your boasted police into believing him French, and his name Noyez. My father is dead, so I may tell the truth, that he served the Kaiser like a loyal subject. And he made a spy of me. I was called to the French colors, and I went, under a French name, but a loyal German at heart! I became a French sub-lieutenant, but I was still a German, and the Kaiser's officers paid me, knew where to find me and how to use me. I must die, but there are yet other agents of the Kaiser distributed through your Army. The Fatherland shall still be served from the French trenches. You will kill me? Bah! My work has already killed at least a regiment of Frenchmen. And since Berger has weakened and betrayed me, I will tell you that he, too, is and always has been a German subject. Remember, there are many more of us wearing the hated uniform of France."

"Noyez! Bamberger!" retorted General Bazain, "I can almost find it in my heart to feel grateful to you, for you have told me that you are not French. Since you are a German I can understand anything. I thank you for assuring me that you are not French."

With a gesture General Bazain ordered the prisoner's removal. Then, his eyes moist, the division commander turned to beckon Dick to him.

"Captain, I have to thank you for finding and helping to remove two dangerous enemies from my command. You will find me grateful—-always!"

Once more outside Lieutenant De Verne turned to Dick to ask:

"You intend returning to the trenches?"

"By all means, for I feel as though the night had but begun," Dick cried. "It has gone well so far, and I am ready for whatever the remaining hours can give me."

"I had hoped that, at the most, you would ask me to find you a bunk in a dug-out where you might sleep," confessed De Verne. "When you have been longer in the trenches, Captain, you will be glad to sleep whenever the chance comes your way."

"But that will not be until I have learned more of the ways of your trench life than I know yet," Dick rejoined. "At present I would rather sleep during the daylight, for it appears to be at night that the real things happen."

De Verne accompanied him back to the fire trench, where Dick was glad to find Captain Ribaut with the other three American officers, that party having returned from a trip down the line.

De Verne soon after took his leave, hastening rearward to begin his rest.

Bang! sounded a field-piece back of the German line.

Between the French first-line and second-line trenches the shell exploded. On the heels of the explosion came a furious burst of discharging artillery.

"This must be what you have been expecting, Major," shouted Ribaut over the racket. "A barrage!"

Down the line ran the noise of bombardment, the thing becoming more furious every instant. Then some shells landed in first-line trenches nearby.

"Take shelter!" shouted Captain Ribaut. "Now! At once!"

French soldiers were scurrying to dug-out shelters. Ribaut led the officer party to a dugout reached by eight descending steps cut in the earth. The apartment in which they found themselves led out some fifteen feet under the barbed wire defenses.

"How long is this likely to last?" demanded Major Wells, eyeing the Frenchman keenly by the light of the one slim candle that burned in the dug-out.

"Perhaps fifteen minutes; maybe until after daylight," Ribaut replied, with a shrug.

"What is the object?"

"Who can say? But a barrage fire is being laid down between our first and second lines. That means that no reinforcements can reach us from the support trenches. And our own trench is being shelled furiously, to drive all into shelters. My friends, it is likely that the Germans, enraged by the capture of Colonel Pernim, who must be missed by now, are paying us back with a raid."

"More of your strenuous doings then, Dick," laughed Greg.

"At least a raid will be highly interesting," Dick retorted. "So far we haven't been in one, and we're here for experience, you know."

"And you really hope that this turns out to be a German raid?" asked Captain Ribaut.

"Yes; don't you, Captain?" challenged Major Wells.

"An, but we French have seen so many of these raids, and they are dull, ugly affairs, sometimes with much killing. After you have seen many you will not hunger for more."

It was not long before conversation was drowned out wholly by the racket of exploding shells in and around the fire trenches. Occasionally one of these drove a jet of sand down the stairs of the dug-out, but this room was too far underground for the dug-out roof to be driven in on them.

Half an hour later the shell-fire against the front-line trenches abated, though the barrage fire still continued to fall between the first and second lines.

Greg whistled softly, unable to hear a note that he emitted. Noll Terry occasionally fingered one of the two gas-masks with which he had been provided before entering the trenches. Major Wells's attitude suggested that he had his ears set to note every difference in sound that came from outside.

A French soldier shouted down the steps in his own tongue:

"Stand by! The Huns are coming!"

At a single bound Captain Ribaut gained the steps and darted up, followed promptly by the American officers.

In the section in which they found themselves four French soldiers, rifles resting over the parapet, stood awaiting the onslaught.

Two more men, equipped with hand bombs, stood awaiting the moment to begin casting.

All the while the curtain of shell-fire, the barrage laid down by the Germans between them and the second-line trenches, continued to fall. It effectually prevented French reinforcements from coming up to the first line.

His automatic pistol ready, Dick Prescott found elbow-room on the fire step. Cautiously he looked over the parapet.

For a moment he could see nothing, save that German shell-fire had blown the barbed wire defenses to pieces, clearing the way for the German invaders to reach them.

In the near distance Dick made out the shadowy figures of the men in the first wave of the German assault.

Rifle-fire began to roll out from the French soldiers. From somewhere at the rear, perhaps from emplacements in or near the French support trenches, the steady drumming of machine-gun fire began. The air was filled with death.

Dick Prescott's blood thrilled with the realization that he was at earnest grip with the Boches!

CHAPTER XIX

In the terrific din of the barrage-fire the men of the first German wave came on like so many silent specters.

They did not run forward, but moved at a fast walk. It was necessary that they save their breath to use in the hand-to-hand struggle that must follow.

Suddenly a French bomb left the trench, striking the ground just in advance of the oncoming Germans. The pink flash of the explosion lighted the set faces of three or four men of the enemy, one of whom went to earth as a fragment from the bomb struck him.

Then bombs fell fast, all along the line. Prescott, singling out an enemy while the flash lasted, let drive at him with a shot from his automatic.

Though several of the Huns fell, the advancing line continued unhesitatingly. The last few steps, past what was left of the barbed wire, the Germans hurled themselves at greater speed.

Then invaders and defenders clashed. German bayonets thrust viciously down into the trench, while French bayonets reached up to dispute them.

Dick had backed away from the fire step. His back against the further wall he was using his automatic pistol to the best advantage.

The first German to leap into the trench landed almost at the feet of Captain Greg Holmes, who had crouched to receive him. Rising, in one of his best old-time football tackles, Greg threw the Hun backward with fearful force, then sat on his chest.

"You're my prisoner!" Holmes shouted at the prostrate. "Try to rise if you dare!"

So hot had been the reception of the first wave that those of the Germans who did not manage to leap down into the trenches, recoiled in dismay.

Then the second wave of raiders came up, only to find that the French had recovered their second wind. Great as the odds were the French held their own, thrusting, shooting and clubbing with rifle butts.

From his position on his prisoner Greg fired coolly as often as he could do so without endangering a French comrade. He longed to rush in closer, but did not intend to let his prisoner get away. Only one German got close enough to thrust at Holmes, who shot him through the heart before the bayonet lunge could be made.

What was left of the first and second waves was being beaten back. Major Wells, Prescott and Noll Terry leaped to the parapet with two French soldiers in their section to beat back the foe.

Just then a third wave arrived. The fighting became brisker. Dick Prescott felt a weight against his head. He staggered dizzily, felt arms clutch at him, and had only a hazy notion of what followed.

The Germans went back, carrying a few prisoners with them. A minute later the enemy barrage lifted.

"You may get up now," Greg admonished his captive, as he leaped to his feet.

"You've accounted for one of the enemy," smiled Captain Ribaut, as he came up.

"Captured him at the first pop out of the box," Holmes declared proudly. "I told him to lie still, and he surely did. I'd have hurt him if he had tried to get away."

"How did you take him?" Ribaut asked, kneeling beside the still man.

"Threw him with an old football tackle."

"The Hun's neck is broken," reported the French captain, raising the enemy's head and letting it fall.

"What's that?" Greg demanded astonished. "Say, you're right, aren't you? And to think of all the good fighting I missed through holding on to that 'prisoner'! Dick will tease the life out of me! By the way, where is he?"

"I thought he went this way," Ribaut answered. "We must find him. I hope he wasn't hurt."

Thoroughly alarmed Greg wheeled and darted along the trench, looking for his chum. Then he raced back, going off in the opposite direction.

"Prescott isn't here!" he gasped, and sprang up at the parapet.

"Here! Don't do that," Major Wells called to him, in a low voice.

But there was no stopping Holmes. Bending low he raced along in front of the trench, looking for the body, dead or alive, of his chum.

Dick, however, was not to be found. Greg continued the search desperately.

Had the Germans sent up flares just then, and turned on their machine guns, Greg would have made an inevitable mark.

Captain Ribaut, more practical, sent a French corporal through the nearby sections for word of Captain Prescott.

"Captain Holmes, return to the trench," Major Wells ordered, in a hoarse whisper.

So Greg obeyed, in time almost to bump into Captain Ribaut.

"Four men from this platoon are missing, and presumably were captured by the enemy," said that officer. "I much fear that Captain Prescott was also taken away by the enemy."

"What? Captured by the Huns?" Greg demanded, divided between amazement and consternation. "Dick captured? Let me lead a force over to the enemy line to bring him back!"

"Only the division commander could sanction that," replied Captain Ribaut, with grave sympathy. "And it is never done, Captain."

"Oh, I wish I had B company at my back, with A company thrown in for good measure!" quivered Greg. "But say, can't there be a mistake? Didn't Prescott go back wounded?"

"No; I have sent to the dressing station, and he was not seen there," Captain Ribaut replied.

At first Greg couldn't believe that his chum had been captured. When the probability of it did dawn on him nothing but his position as an officer kept him from sitting down on the fire step and sobbing.

"I'd sooner know he was killed than that he had fallen into Hun hands," Holmes sputtered. "But, if they have got him, then I'll make a business of mistreating Germans after this!"

Capture was precisely what had happened to Dick Prescott. It was not for long that he had remained dazed. Two German soldiers fairly dragged him across No Man's Land, his heels bumping over the rough ground.

Dick vaguely knew when the same men lifted him slightly and dropped him, feet first, into the German trench. He fell forward to his knees, and a German non-com raised him to his feet.

"What place is this?" Dick demanded. But he knew as soon as he heard laughing German voices around him.

"Well, if I'm captured, I gave a good account of myself first," Prescott muttered as he shook himself together, "I first captured two German spies and a German colonel and turned them over to the French. But poor old Greg! I'd almost sooner be in my present boots than in his, for he'll be frantic when he finds this out."

The same two German soldiers who had dragged him across No Man's Land were now permitted the honor of piloting their distinguished captive back from the line. Leading him into a communication trench, they started with him for the rear.

Though he still felt dizzy, Dick found his head clearing as he moved along. He was able to judge that he had walked half a mile through the communication trench, then at least another half-mile along a road before he was halted at a hole in the ground.

"Go down here," said one of the men in German, and pushed Dick down a long flight of steps, leading to a large, electrically lighted dug-out at least twenty-five feet below the earth's surface.

"Only prisoners of rank received here, without orders," said a sergeant near the foot of the stairs.

"But this man is a captain," returned one of the captors.

"Of what army?"

"The American."

"Bring the prisoner here!" ordered a voice from the further end of the underground room.

Dick was hustled along, bringing up at last in front of a long table, behind which sat three German officers.

"You are an American?" asked the officer who sat between the other two. He spoke in English.

"Yes," Dick admitted.

"Of what regiment?" demanded the questioner.

"Infantry regiment," Dick replied.

"Yes, but how is your regiment known?"

"As an infantry regiment," Dick answered, though he knew well what was wanted of him.

"Are your American regiments numbered?"

"Oh, yes."

"How is yours numbered?"

"Numbered among the best, I believe," Dick returned, with a smile.

"You are a captain?"

"Yes."

"Then you know what I mean to ask, and you must not try to trifle with me. How is your regiment numbered? What is the number of your regiment?"

"Numbered among the best, as I told you."

"How long have you been in France?"

"Long enough to like its people, meaning those who belong here, not those who have come into France by force of arms."

"Captain, is your regiment on the line yet?"

"It's a line regiment, of course," Prescott replied dumbly.

"Captain," spoke the questioner angrily, "you must not try to make game of us! If you do not answer our questions you will regret it."

"And if I did answer them I'd feel ashamed of myself," Dick smiled blandly. "I'm going to take the liberty of asking you a question. If you were captured and questioned, how much would you tell that would injure Germany?"

"I'd tell nothing," replied the German officer stiffly.

"Same here," Dick went on smilingly. "I'm as strong for my country as you are for yours."

"But, Captain, you will have to tell us your name and rank, also the designation of your organization. That has to be entered on our records."

"I am Captain Richard Prescott, captain of infantry, United States Army," Dick returned, in a business-like way. "But when you go further, and ask me for information about the American Army, you need expect no sensible answers."

"Take this man to the temporary prisoners' camp, and see that he is put in the officers' section," said the questioner to the two guards who had brought Dick in.

So Dick was led out again, and once more escorted along a road. He judged that the walk from dug-out to camp must have been at least two miles in length. The "prison" to which he found himself taken consisted of a high barbed wire enclosure, with a small wooden building at one end, and another end of the enclosure fenced off for officers.

Into the building Dick was taken first. It contained only one room and was evidently used as a booking and record office.

Again he was asked his name by an officer behind a desk. As before Prescott refused to state anything further than that his name was Richard Prescott, and that he was a captain of infantry in the American Army.

"But you will have to tell us more than that," objected the German officer blandly.

"I'll answer any questions you may put to me," promised Dick, "but I won't agree, in advance, to answer them truthfully."

Another bald effort was made to force him to answer questions, but Dick gave evasive replies that carried no information.

"Take the fellow to the officers' section," ordered the man at the desk, at last.

So through a dark yard Prescott was led between rows of prisoners sleeping on the ground. Some of them, too cold and miserable to sleep, stirred uneasily as the newcomers passed by.

It was the same in the officers' section. Though the night was cold, all prisoners were sleeping on bare ground in the open.

There were some four hundred prisoners in this lot, all French except Prescott.

In the officers' section he found some twenty men, also all French. Two of them sat up as Dick entered.

"Hola!" cried one of them in his own tongue. "You are an American?"

"Yes," Prescott admitted.

"Come and join us. We have the best bed in this camp."

"It looks as if it might be hard," smiled Dick, glancing down at the men.

"Hard, but not so bad, after all," replied the other officer.
"See, we have removed our overcoats and spread them on the ground. And we have two blankets over us. Come under the blankets with us, and we shall all be warmer."

Dick hesitated. He wondered if he wouldn't be crowding them out of their none too good protection against the night air.

"If you get in with us," urged the first, "it will make us all warmer."

On the face of it that looked reasonable, provided he did not crowd either out under the edge of the blankets.

"Oh, there will be plenty of room," one of them assured him. "We can lie very close together. And you have no blanket if you sleep by yourself."

So Dick allowed himself to be persuaded. Then, to his surprise, they insisted that he get in the middle between them. This, too, he finally accepted, but repaid them in part by taking off his trench coat and spreading it over the blankets in such a way that all three gained added warmth from it.

"How long have you been here?" Dick asked.

"Two weeks," replied one of the pair. "It is a wretched life. Had I known how bad it was I would have forced my captors to kill me."

That was cheering news, indeed!

"We must sleep now," spoke the other officer. "There is little sleep be to had here in the daytime, and then we can talk."

Dick lay awake a long time. A prisoner in the hands of the Huns! All he had heard of the wretched treatment accorded prisoners by the Germans came back to him. At least he had the satisfaction of knowing that he was not a prisoner through any act of his own.

CHAPTER XX

At last he fell asleep. When he awoke the sun was shining in his face. He was alone, for his bed-fellows of the night were already astir. They had tucked him in as warmly as possible before leaving him.

Closing his eyes, Dick slumbered again. When he next opened his eyes he sat up.

"Good morning, comrade!" called one of the two between whom he had slept.

"Ah, good morning," Prescott answered in French, and stood up.
"My, but the mattress in this bed is a beastly one."

The officer who addressed him, a young man of twenty-five or so, laughed good-humoredly.

"What time is breakfast to be had here?" Dick asked.

"I fear, comrade, that we shall not have any this morning, for the news is that we are to be entrained to-day and sent away."

"To Germany?"

"It must be. And on embarkation mornings no food is served."

"They start us away hungry?" Dick asked.

"Always, so I have been told. But you are not missing much, comrade, for you are not yet accustomed to the food the Germans feed their prisoners, and no one eats much of it until he has been hungry for a few days. Then something like an appetite for the stuff comes to one."

Finding himself somewhat chilled and cramped Prescott began to go briskly through some of the Army setting-up exercises.

"That is a fine thing to warm the blood," said one of the French officers, "but I warn you that it will make you hungry."

The other French officers now came forward to make themselves known to the only American officer in this prison camp.

"We are moving to-day," said one. "Will it be better in the new prison than here, do you think?" Prescott asked.

"In some ways at least. We shall undoubtedly be housed in a wooden building, and that should be warmer at night. Besides, I hear we are permitted

112

straw mattresses when in Germany."

"That begins to sound like luxury," laughed Dick.

"And there our friends can send us food through neutral agencies."

"Do you suppose, if they do, we shall be allowed to have some of the food?" Dick asked.

"Some of it, at least, or our friends would quickly stop sending it to us when they heard from us that we did not get it."

"It will be a dog's life," broke in another, "even with such better treatment as may be accorded to officers."

Dick Prescott's heart was as stout as any American's heart could be, but as he listened to the talk of his French brothers in arms he could not help feeling glum.

For one thing, it was hardly for this that he had sailed from America to be taken at the outset and to be shut off from all service with the men of his own country!

A German under-officer who spoke French came to the wire to call out:

"You officers will march from here soon. Begin to get your packs ready. There must be no delay."

"It won't take me long," Dick told his new friends. "When captured I had only my uniform and my pistol. The latter was taken."

He turned to, however, to help his French brothers who possessed blankets, water bottles and other small belongings, for some of them appeared almost too weak to prepare for the march.

The same order had been given to the enlisted men in the next enclosure. For a few minutes there was some bustle over getting petty belongings together and marshaling them into a pack that could be slung over the back.

"Officers ready!" ordered the under-officer, returning. "Fall in by twos and march after me to the office."

He marched the little detachment through the larger enclosure, and in through the rear of the office building. Here there was a roll-call. Then the officers, again in twos, were marched outside, where a corporal and four soldiers fell in with them as guard.

Down the road the captured officers were marched for something like a quarter of a mile.

"Halt, but keep your places in the ranks," ordered the corporal.

"Any prisoner disobeying will be shot."

"There is something that promises!" cried Captain Lescault, pointing to the sky.

Southward, over the lines, appeared a squadron of swift French airplanes, coming over the German lines. Almost instantly German aircraft began to rise from the ground, going to meet the invaders of the air.

Over the purring of the engines sounded the sharp, continuous rapping of machine guns as the opposing craft fought each other.

Two German planes came crashing down to earth. More appeared in the air, until the French flyers, outnumbered, turned and flew back over the French lines.

"I believe our flyers got what they wanted," whispered the same French officer to Prescott.

Five minutes later the Frenchman whispered exultingly:

"Ah, I was sure of it! Our airmen were spying for the artillery. Now you shall see things happen."

In the air sounded a screech. Then, less than three hundred yards further down the road a French shell exploded, overturning a motor truck and killing both Germans on its seat. The truck itself was a wreck.

Crash! Another shell landed in the road, bowling over two officers at the head of a body of oncoming soldiers. The next shell landed in a mass of marching German infantry, killing and wounding several. Then, for five minutes a hurricane of shells descended on that road, wrecking trucks, killing and wounding more than a hundred men in German marching detachments, and chasing all troops from the road.

"That does not win the war!" growled the German corporal in charge of the officer-prisoners. "It is only French mischief!"

Hardly had the shell hurricane ceased when some hundred men, under guard, came marching down from the prison camp. These were halted, at the edge of the field, just behind the officers.

An hour passed before another detachment of prisoners was marched down the road and halted. Later more came. Noon had passed before the final detachment arrived.

It was wearisome, but Dick Prescott did not feel that he had wasted his time. Full of the hope of escaping, some day, he had watched covertly everything that he could see of German army life and movements behind the fighting line. Also, from several incidents that he witnessed, he gained a new idea of German military brutality.

One scene that made his blood boil was when a French officer, a wounded man, and suffering also from hunger, let himself slide to a sitting posture on the ground.

"Here, you!" ordered the German corporal advancing threateningly. "You have been told that you must stand in line."

"But our comrade is weak from loss of blood," interposed another French officer who spoke German.

"Take that for your meddling," retorted the corporal, landing the back of his hand stingingly on his informant's face. It was a humiliating blow, that a prisoner could not resent in kind.

"Get up," ordered the corporal, "or I shall aid you with my bayonet."

Though the words were not understood by the sufferer, the gesture was. He tried to obey, but did not rise fast enough to suit the corporal.

"Here," mocked the fellow. "That will help you!"

His bayonet point passed through the seat of the victim's trousers, more than pricking the flesh inside.

"Coward!" hissed Prescott and three of four of the French officers.

"If you don't like it, and are not civil," raged the corporal hoarsely, "I shall beat some of you with the butt of my gun."

Subsequently a French officer who had stepped a foot further than he was supposed to stand was rebuked by the corporal's gun-butt striking him on the knee-cap. After that the prisoner limped.

"These brutes ought to be killed—-every one of them!" Dick muttered disgustedly to a French officer near him.

"Most of them will be, before this long war is over," nodded the Frenchman, "but a soldier's death is too fine for such beasts."

Finally a German officer arrived. Under his crisp orders the now long column of prisoners moved out into the road, forming compactly and guarded by at least forty infantrymen. The order to march was given. With only two halts the prisoners were marched some eight miles, arriving late in the afternoon at a railway yard.

Here the column was halted again for an hour, while the German officer was absent, presumably, in search of his orders. When the march was taken up again its course led across a network of tracks to a long train.

"Why, these are cattle cars," uttered Prescott, disgustedly, when the column had been halted along the length of the foremost part of the train. "And, judging by the odor, these cars haven't been cleaned."

"They won't be until we are through riding in them," returned the French officer at his side. "This is what comes to soldiers who surrender to the German dogs!"

Only one car was given over to the officer-prisoners, who were forced to climb into the unsavory car through a side door. No seats had been provided, but there was not more than room to stand up in the stuffy car. Fortunately the spaces between the timbers of the car sides gave abundant ventilation.

Into cars to the rear the enlisted prisoners were packed. To stomachs that had been empty of food all day the odors were especially distressing.

As the officer in charge of the prisoners came to the side door of the first car Dick made bold to prefer a request.

"We have had no water all day. May we have a bucket of it in here before the train starts?"

"There will not be time," replied the German officer coldly, and moved away. Yet two hours passed, and the train did not start.

Suddenly German guns behind the front, along a stretch of miles, opened a heavy bombardment. Dick and his French friends gazed out at a sky made violently lurid by the reflection of the flashes of these great pieces. Then the French guns answered furiously, nor did all the French shells fall upon the German trenches or batteries. The French knew the location of this railway yard. Within twenty minutes five hundred large caliber shells had fallen in or near this yard. Freight and passenger coaches were struck and splintered.

Into the forward cattle car bounded the corporal who had tormented them that day. Behind him, in the doorway, appeared the German officer.

"Count the prisoners," ordered the latter, "and make sure that all are there. We are going to pull out of here before those crazy French yonder destroy all our rolling stock."

Fifteen minutes later, though the French shell-fire had ceased coming this way, the train crawled out of the yard. It ran along slowly, though sometime in the night it increased its speed.

Dick Prescott will never forget the misery of that night. When the train was under way the cold was intense in these half-open cattle cars. No appeal for water to drink was heeded.

Despite their discomforts, most of the prisoners managed to sleep some, though standing up.

In the middle of the night Prescott awoke, stiff, nauseated, hungry and parched with tormenting thirst. Though he did not know it at that moment, the train had halted because of a breakdown in a train ahead.

Along the track came that tormenting corporal. While a soldier held up a dim lantern the corporal unlocked the padlock, sliding the side door back.

At that moment an order was bawled lustily in German.

"Will you be good enough to repeat, Herr Lieutenant?" called the corporal, glancing backward down the length of train.

Heavy footsteps were heard approaching. Corporal and private turned to take a few steps back to meet their officer. Dick, standing in the open doorway, saw that a fog had settled down over the night.

Acting on a sudden impulse, without an instant's hesitation, he leaped down, striking softly on the balls of his feet. Without even turning sideways to see if German eyes had observed him, Prescott stole across another track, and down to the foot of an embankment.

"They'll shoot me for this!" he muttered. "Let them! Death is better than being a German prisoner!"

CHAPTER XXI

SEEKING DEATH MORE THAN ESCAPE

In another instant the French officer who had been standing next to Dick attempted the same trick. He had just gained the ground when the German lieutenant, turning his gaze from the corporal's face, and glancing ahead, broke off in the middle of his instructions to cry out:

"There's a prisoner escaping! Halt him or shoot him!"

Realizing that he was hopelessly caught, and trusting to better luck next time, the Frenchman held up his hands.

"Get back into the car," ordered the German lieutenant. "Corporal, take the lantern and see that all the prisoners are in there."

As the corporal obeyed, the lieutenant looked in and nodded.

"There was no time for any to escape," he remarked. "We nipped the first one. You are scoundrels when you try to disgrace me by escaping. Just for the attempt of this comrade of yours, gentlemen, you shall have no breakfast in the morning."

The door was moved quickly into place, the padlock snapped, and then the guard turned to other matters.

Not a French officer in that car but would sooner have died than betray the fact that Dick had slipped out of sight. Though they themselves were still in the car, they prayed that he might find either safety from the Germans, or that better thing than captivity, death.

As for Captain Prescott, he had slipped into a field beyond. When he halted to peer about he was perhaps sixty feet from the train. Moving cautiously he made the distance another hundred feet. Yet he did not dare to go far at present, nor rapidly.

"I'm out of the car, if nothing more," Dick reflected, inhaling a deep breath of the foggy air. "I shall always feel grateful to that German engineer. His blowing off steam made noise enough so that my jump and my footsteps weren't heard."

One of Dick's feet, moving exploringly, touched a stone. Bending over and groping, he found three fair-sized stones.

"Good enough!" he thought, picking them up. "Sooner or later, to-night, wandering around in an American uniform, I'm going to be heard and halted. I'll throw these stones at the sentry who tries to halt me, and then he'll fire. After he shoots there'll be no German prison ahead for me!"

This wasn't exactly a thought in the cheerful class, yet Prescott smiled. More contented with his prospects he moved softly away.

For the first hundred feet from the embankment his shoes touched grass. Then he came to the edge of a ploughed field. Here he felt that he must proceed with even greater caution, for now most of the train noises had ceased and he feared to slip or stumble, and thus make a noise that might be carried on the still night air to the ears of the train guard.

However, he soon struck a smooth path leading through the ploughed ground, and now moved along a little faster.

"This is just where caution ought to pay big dividends," he told himself. "A path is usually made to lead to where human beings live and congregate. I'll stop every few feet and listen."

The first sound that came to his ears from out of the veiled distance ahead made the young American officer almost laugh aloud. It was the crowing of a rooster.

"If you know how hungry I am, my bird, I doubt if you'd make any noise to draw me your way."

However, the crowing had given him a valuable clew, for he reasoned that the barnyard home of Mr. Rooster must be near the general buildings of a farm. These buildings he decided to avoid. So, when he came to a fork in the path he chose the direction that led him further from what he believed to be the location of the farm buildings.

By this time he was moving more rapidly, though striving to make no noise in moving. Suddenly he came to a road and stopped, gasping.

"I don't want anything as public as this," Dick told himself. "Troops use roads. However, as I've reached the road, and want to get as far from the train as possible, I believe I'll take a look from the other side of the road. There may be a field there better suited to my needs."

Directly opposite, at the other edge of the road, two tree trunks reared themselves close together, looking tall and gaunt against the white of the fog. After listening a moment Dick started to cross the road to them.

Just as he reached the trunks he saw something move around the further one, and drew back quickly. It was well that he did so, for the moving thing was a man armed with an axe which he had swung high and now tried to bring

119

down relentlessly on Prescott's head.

But Dick's arms shot up, his hands catching the haft and wrenching the ugly weapon away from its wielder.

"No, you don't!" Dick muttered in English, taking another step backward from the wild-looking old peasant who had attempted to brain him.

"But a thousand pardons, monsieur!" cried the old man hoarsely in French, and now shaking from head to foot. "I did not see well in the fog, and I mistook you for a German. You are a British soldier!"

"An American soldier," Dick replied in the same tongue.

"Then, had I killed you, grief would have killed me, too, as it has already sent my wits scattering. For I am a Frenchman and hate only Germans."

"Is this a safe place to stand and discuss the Germans?" asked Dick mildly, in a voice barely above a whisper. "This road——"

"No, no! It is not safe here," protested the peasant. "Soldiers and wagons move over this road. That was why I was here. I hoped to find some German soldier alone, to leap on him and kill him——and I thought you a German until after I had swung at you. Heaven is good, and I have not to reproach myself for having struck at the American uniform. But you are in danger here. You are——"

"An escaped prisoner," Dick supplied in a whisper. "I have just escaped from the Germans."

"If you are quick then, they shall not find you," promised the old man, seizing Dick by the arm. "Come! I can guide you even through this fog."

There was something so sincere about the old peasant, despite his wildness, that Prescott went with him without objection. Both moving softly, they stepped into another field, the guide going forward as one who knew every inch of the way.

Presently buildings appeared faintly in the fog.

"Wait here," whispered the peasant, and was gone. He soon came back.

"There are no German soldiers about the place," the old man informed Dick. "I will take you into the house——hide you. You shall have food and drink!"

Food and something to drink! To Dick Prescott, at that moment, this sounded like a promise of bliss.

To a rear door the old man led the American, and inside, closing and bolting the door after him. Here the man struck a light, and a candle shed its rays over a well-kept kitchen.

As Dick laid the axe down in a corner he heard a sobbing sound from a room nearby.

"It is the dear old wife," said the peasant, in an awed tone. "To-day the German monsters took our son and our daughter, and marched them off with other young people from the village. They have been taken to Germany to toil as slaves of the wild beasts. Do you wonder, monsieur, that the good wife sobs and that I haunted the road hoping to find a German soldier alone and to slay him? But I must hide you, for Germans might come here at any moment."

Throwing open a door the old man revealed a flight of stairs. He led the way to a room above. Here a door cunningly concealed behind a dresser was opened after the guide had moved the dresser. At a sign Dick entered the other room, only to find himself confronted by another man, whose face, revealed by the candle light, caused Captain Dick Prescott to recoil as though from a ghost.

CHAPTER XXII

CAN IT BE THE OLD CHUM?

"You know each other?" cried the old peasant, as he observed the amazement of two young men. "You are enemies?"

As he saw the pair fairly hug each other he added hastily:

"But no! You are friends!"

Then he added, as if he were saying something new:

"Friends, quite certainly."

"You, Dick Prescott!" gasped the other young man.

"Tom Reade!" uttered the young captain delightedly.

The old peasant held the candle higher that he might see better what was taking place. In that light Dick made another discovery.

"Tom, you're in uniform! Aviation service, at that!"

"What else did you expect?" Tom demanded. "Especially after I wrote and told you all about it."

"When?"

"Last July."

"Where did you send the letter?"

"To you at Camp Baker."

"It was in July that we left Camp Baker for Camp Berry. Your letter must have gone astray. I heard from the old home town of Gridley that you and Hazelton had gone across—-something to do with welfare work. I couldn't make it out," Dick hurried on," neither did I know where to address you."

"That's just it, though!" exclaimed Tom Reade, with a happy laugh. "Welfare work explains it to a dot. We're working for the welfare of the world by helping to kill as many Huns as possible!"

"But how came you to be here?"

"I might ask as much of you, Dick, as you and I appear to be in exactly the same boat."

It looked rather ungrateful toward the old peasant who had brought these old,

old friends together, but for a few moments both forgot him. When they remembered him they found that the old man had gone, closing the door.

Then Dick told what had befallen him, after which Reade explained that, three nights before, on a night flight over the German lines, his plane had been damaged by a fragment of shell from an anti-aircraft gun. Reade had been obliged to descend some forty miles behind the German front lines. Fortunately he had come down in a field near the house in which he now hid. He had cautiously come to this house, and as cautiously aroused the inmates, reasoning that they must be French and should befriend him. This the peasants had cheerfully done.

"I've been hiding here since, and my machine was found, but I wasn't," Tom wound up.

"You see, this room has no windows, and I keep very quiet, and so, perhaps, I could remain here safely a month. But I won't. I have plans for escape back to the French lines."

At this moment the door opened again. The old peasant came in with a tray on which was a dish of smoking meat, dark bread and potatoes and a pot of coffee.

"Now, since you are old friends I shall leave you," said the old man smiling, as he patted both young Americans on the shoulder. "But Monsieur Reade knows how to call me if I am wanted. Good rest and stout hearts, young gentlemen!"

"We'll feast a bit!" cried Prescott eagerly.

"You will," Tom corrected. "I've had my evening meal and am not hungry. Eat before the candle burns out, and while you do so I will fix the ventilator for the night. When you have eaten we can turn in on the bed, for we can talk there as well as when sitting in the dark." Dick fell to ravenously on the food and coffee, while Tom attended to ventilation by removing a loose brick from a chimney, half of which was in this blind attic.

"We must pay this peasant well," Dick proposed, when he had nearly finished the meal, "for I'll wager he is not rich."

"I can pay him all right," declared Reade, striking a hand against his waist-line. "In my money belt I have a stock of American gold. Gold is a money that is very popular in Europe in these days of hardship."

Later the chums disrobed and turned in. There was abundance of covering to the bed.

"Now," proposed Tom Reade, talking in whispers, "for my plan of escape. It's dangerous, and it sounds impossible, fantastic. But now that you're here, Dick Prescott, I feel equal to putting anything through! So here's for the plan!"

It was dangerous enough, certainly, as Tom Reade outlined it. It didn't even strike Captain Prescott as being possible of performance, but he didn't say so. It was the only plan of escape that presented itself, and Tom had evidently put in all his hopes on that idea.

From the plan the chums fell to talking of other days. In the end, however, their whispers became more indistinct, then died out. Both were asleep.

Dick, as he slumbered and tossed, still felt the motion of that hideous prison train, but at last fell into deep slumber.

When he finally awoke he beheld Tom Reade, fully dressed in his uniform, seated at some distance under a little opening in the roof, reading a book.

"Awake, eh?" asked Tom, when he heard his chum stir. After glancing at his wrist watch, he added:

"You've slept nine hours and a half, and I guess you needed it. There is water for washing, and I'll consult our host about breakfast. What do you think of this way of letting in daylight? Toward night I shove this black cover over the hole in the roof, so that candle light may not show through the roof and give us away to the Germans."

Stepping to the chimney, from which the "ventilator" brick was still absent, Reade put his hand inside, finding a cord and giving it a gentle tug.

By the time that Prescott was partly dressed the door opened and the old peasant looked in.

"We are wondering what you can give us for breakfast?" Tom said in French. "Are eggs to be had to-day? Omelettes?"

"Yes, I can get eggs," nodded the old man.

"As you've not seen the color of my money yet," Tom continued, "please take this on account."

At first the old peasant hung back from accepting the proffered gold coin, though at last he took it, remarking:

"I will admit that I am poor, and yet it seems a crime to accept money from an American."

Half an hour later their host returned, bringing two hot omelettes, dark bread, potatoes and the inevitable pot of coffee.

"It is with difficulty that we keep food hidden," he murmured, in a low voice.

"A dozen times the Huns have appeared and have taken from us all the food they could find. But we still have flour, potatoes and coffee hidden where they cannot find them. We shall hope to continue to exist until you Americans have helped drive the Hun from our land."

From the nearby road came the sound of moving trucks. The old man paused and shook his fist in the direction of the sound. After he had served the breakfast he climbed upon a stool, putting his eyes to the hole in the sloping roof and peering toward the road.

"Ah, the vermin!" he hissed. "A regiment of their accursed infantry marching toward the front. Oh, that your men and ours might kill them all this day!"

"Give us time, and we'll do it," Tom promised unconcernedly.

After breakfast the two chums talked almost without stopping until it was time for luncheon. In the afternoon Tom stretched, then walked toward the bed, declaring:

"When one has no chance to exercise I believe sleep to be the next best thing, even extra sleep. I believe that I can sleep until supper time. And after that— perhaps it will be tonight, Dick, that we make our fantastic effort to place ourselves on the other side of the German battle front!"

"The sooner the better," cried Dick, "only provided that speed does not waste our chance to escape."

"If we must go down in defeat," yawned Reade, "I believe we may at least look for the satisfaction of carrying a few Huns with us. I believe I have forgotten to mention the fact that I have my automatic pistol with me. It's hidden, but I could show it to you."

"I'm glad you have it," murmured Dick, as he closed his eyes. "I never before felt the desire to slay human beings, but since I've struck the French front I've had a constant desire to kill Huns!"

"To-night, then," said Reade drowsily, "we may find the chance both to kill Huns and get back to the French lines."

CHAPTER XXIII

THE DASH TO GET BACK TO PERSHING

"After dark, by a whole hour!" whispered Reade, after waking, striking a match and looking at his wrist watch. "Hustle, Dick!"

Tom's next act was to light a candle. "Want supper?" he asked.

"I could eat it," Prescott replied. "But what's the use?"

"What do you mean?"

"Why waste time with eating when there's the slimmest chance to get away?" Dick continued.

"It may be hours before we can really put our plan into execution."

"Our plan?" repeated Dick. "What on earth did I have to do with making the plan? But, if you feel that we're not wasting time over a supper I'll admit that I am ready to eat."

So Reade summoned their host, as before.

"Is the night good and foggy?" Tom asked, when the aged peasant appeared.

"There is not a trace of fog, monsieur," was the reply. "Still, the sky is cloudy, and the night is dark."

"That's only second-best weather," grumbled Reade. "However, I'm impatient to have a try to-night. I think we will try for it. Can you help us?"

"Undoubtedly I can find out how clear the coast is," replied the old man. "I would be glad to do far more than that for you."

"If you can supply us with supper," Tom proposed, "and then find out the news, it will be a great service."

Later, while the chums ate, the old peasant went abroad. Tom and Dick were waiting impatiently until he returned.

"All is as well as it will be any night," the Frenchman reported, and added details.

"We'll try it, then," Reade decided, after glancing at Prescott, who nodded.

"And may you succeed!" cried the old peasant fervently. "And may you both come safely through the war, and have the good fortune to slay Huns and Huns and Huns!"

"Promise me, my good old friend, to use your axe only for chopping wood," Dick urged,

"And I will promise to think of you whenever I have the chance to destroy a Hun."

"It is a bargain, then!" cried their host.

"It will be kept, on my side," Dick rejoined gravely.

"And on mine, too," agreed the old man.

It was quiet abroad when the three stealthily left the house. The Americans had wished to leave a word of cheer with the peasant's wife, but she had fallen asleep and they would not disturb her.

Through a wood and across fields their guide led the young Americans until they neared the spot they sought.

"From here on one will have to be cautious," suggested the Frenchman. "You are about to cross a road, and then, on the other side, one comes to the aviation station."

"Then here is where you should leave us," Dick remarked considerately. "Very likely we shall fail and be sent on to a prison camp, this time in irons. Perhaps we shall be shot. But we do not care to let an old man, and a Frenchman follow us to a death that he should not invite."

"I would go with you until I see you safely in sight of the station," objected the Frenchman.

"It seems unnecessary, and contemptible in us to risk your life along with our own. Do you understand the lay of the land, Tom? Can you find our objective without risking the life of our good old friend here?"

"I am sure that I can," Reade nodded. "Like yourself, Dick, I feel that he should not come further with us. And see here, monsieur. You have not asked our names, neither have we known yours. Some day, when all around here is French territory again, and the beastly German has gone forever, we shall want to look you up, or write you. I am Lieutenant Tom Reade, of the American aviation service, and my friend is Captain Richard Prescott, of the American Infantry."

"And I am Francois Prim. My neighbors call me Papa Prim."

"Show us the way we are to go, Monsieur Prim," Dick urged.

"It is simple," replied Papa Prim. "You see, without fail, the little building to which I am pointing, over by the roadside?"

"Yes."

"That was our school-house. Now it is an office for the Prussians. They have a battalion or more of infantry camped in the field across from the building. They are a guard to keep us afraid. Sometimes one will see three or four regiments camped further along on that field, either regiments going to the front or coming back for rest. Now, from that building you turn and go in that direction"—-Papa Prim made a motion with his crooked forefinger——"and so you come to four sheds that are easily missed in the night, for they are camouflaged so as not to attract the eye of French flyers in the day time. From here it will be the first shed that you come to that is more likely to be open at night. In each shed are two airplanes. They are kept here for the purpose of sending up at night when French planes pass over to bomb railways or perhaps to bomb German towns. When our own French airmen come then these airplanes shoot up into the sky and give battle. But the Huns have lost twelve planes here in half that number of months," Papa Prim added proudly, "and only lately have enough new ones arrived from Germany to make up the eight required for this station."

"Where do the airmen sleep?" Dick interjected.

"In the camp with the troops; in the hangars there are no sleeping places."

"And the hangars are at some distance from the troop camp?" Tom asked.

"The troop camp begins over that way," Papa Prim continued, pointing, "for, as you will understand, there must be ground on which the airplanes may run before they rise. So there is some distance. I came near forgetting to tell you that, behind the hangars, are four tents in which the hangar guard sleeps."

"And how many sentries at a time walk post around the hangars?" Dick inquired.

"I do not know," confessed Papa Prim, "but I do not believe there are more than three or four sentries on duty at a time. Of course, there are other sentries on post at the camp."

"And airships leaving fly directly over the camp?" Tom wanted to know.

"You have said truly," replied Papa Prim. "And are there anti-aircraft guns in the camp?" Tom asked.

"In the troop camp, so I have heard, but I have not seen them," answered Papa Prim.

Removing his steel helmet and taking it in his left hand, Dick bent over, seizing Papa Prim's hand.

"Good-bye for a little while, monsieur," he said earnestly. "We go away with hearts full of gratitude to your own fine, loyal heart. May you prosper and be happy, with your children safely returned from Germany. May all good things in life be with you. Our thanks will always be with you, and our thoughts often of you, monsieur."

Tom Reade took leave of Papa Prim in equally hearty and grateful words.

The two Americans watched the slim, bent old figure plodding homeward. After looking the ground over critically, they stole forward on their way.

"I didn't want him to see what disagreeable business we may have on our hands within a few minutes," Dick whispered. "But see here, Tom, I've just remembered that you didn't pay Papa Prim for all his trouble, as you had planned."

"Didn't I?" Reade chuckled. "I did it without any dispute from him, either. Dick, I wrapped five twenty-dollar American gold pieces in cloth, so they wouldn't jingle, and stuffed the whole tightly into a small canvas bag. While you were talking I slipped it into one of his blouse pockets. Papa Prim will find the money there, and he'll know who put it there, but he won't be able to return it."

"American gold?" Dick echoed. "If the Germans ever know of his having American gold they'll think it reason enough for hanging him."

"No, they won't," Tom retorted, "though they would undoubtedly think it reason enough for taking the money away from him. But I've seen plenty of American gold in France, and plenty of English gold, too. Anywhere in the world gold is gold, and having American gold isn't proof, during this war, that the possessor got it from an American. I'll wager that there is plenty of American gold locked up even in Germany. But the Germans will never find Papa's gold. Papa Prim will hide it until the day comes when, like the good Frenchman that he is, he can turn that gold into a French war bond."

Nearing the former school-house that had been pointed out to them, the two chums took their bearings afresh. Crossing the road one at a time, with utmost stealth, they reached the other side without having been challenged.

A little further on they espied a German sentry, pacing post. Waiting until the fellow had gone to the furthest limit of his post, the chums, flat on their stomachs, crawled forward until, on looking backward, they judged it safe to rise and move on crouchingly. Then they came in sight of the aviation station.

"Better crawl all the way now," Dick whispered. "We have reached the point where any attempt at speed will be sure to place a few bullets in our bodies."

Tom nodded, without speaking. It was trampled, withered grass through which they now crawled. It offered fair concealment, but there was danger of making a noise that might betray them to a keen-eared sentry.

At last, near the first hangar, they reached a spot where two trees stood close together. Crawling to this shelter, they still remained lying down, though the tree trunks gave them greater safety against being seen.

In front of the hangars paced a sentry; at the rear another soldier walked post. At some distance from this latter sentry stood four tents, in which, Papa Prim had declared, slept the reliefs of the guard.

"I see how we could get the sentry at the rear," Dick whispered, after a few minutes' silent survey. "But it's at the front that we want to get in, and I don't see any way of creeping up on the front sentry without the rear sentry seeing us and firing. That would give the alarm."

"Then we've got to 'get' the rear sentry first?" Tom asked, his lips at his chum's ear.

"That's it."

"Nasty business, and double chance of losing the game."

"It's the only way, Tom, unless your head is working better than mine."

For some minutes Tom Reade studied.

"I guess it will have to be the rear sentry first," he conceded.

At that moment a small door at the rear of the hangar opened.
The two friends heard the noise, and judged by sound more than sight.

"Sentry!" said the man who had stepped outside, in a low voice.

"Herr Lieutenant!" responded the man. "I am not locking the door, sentry. I shall be back before long."

"Very good, Herr Lieutenant." Passing to the front of the hangar this German aviation lieutenant waited until the sentry there had reached him, then delivered the same information, after which the aviation officer strode off briskly toward the troop camp that could be only vaguely seen in the distance.

"It sounds as if he intended to make a flight," whispered Dick uneasily.

"That wouldn't be so bad," Reade replied. "It will be worse if his machine is out of order and he is coming back to fuss over it."

"We must make our break now," Prescott whispered.

"Lead the way," answered Reade. Fortunately, at this moment, the sentries were at the outer ends of their posts. Bending low, keeping his gaze on the sentries, Dick scurried noiselessly over the ground until he paused, erect and panting, under the shadow of the building near the rear.

So far safe, for Reade was with him an instant later. While the rear sentry finished his post at this end just beyond the hangar, the front sentry, as far as had been observed, came only as far as the sliding doors of the hangar.

"Get your automatic ready!" Dick whispered. Then they heard the rear sentry coming toward them.

There came that tense instant when the sentry's passing form loomed up within three feet of Captain Prescott. Losing not an instant Dick sprang upon him with the bound of a panther.

There was no outcry, for Dick's fingers sought and found the fellow's throat, encircling it. Wrenching the enemy soldier off his balance, Prescott laid him low, the man's bayoneted rifle falling across his body.

It was Dick's eyes that said, "Ready, Tom!" Reade hesitated for a second or so, then struck the prostrate, choking enemy between the eyes. It was a fearful blow, and the man collapsed.

"One down, but we must get the other!" Dick whispered sternly.

They stole forward along the side of the building, Dick in the lead. Peeping around the corner he saw the sentry almost finishing the nearer end of his post. Back came Prescott's head like a shot. He waited until he knew by the tread that the sentry had turned and was going back over his post. Then it was that Dick stole upon him from behind. Another leap, a grip around the man's throat, and sentry number two was on his back, where Reade gave him the grace blow.

Without a word the chums picked up this sentry, carrying him around to the rear. Then Dick sought the small rear door of the hangar. It opened softly, and they entered, closing it behind them.

All was darkness in here until Reade, producing his pocket electric torch, threw a beam of light over the scene.

While Dick stood still, now holding the automatic pistol, Tom took a rapid look over each of the two air machines.

"This nearer one looks like the newer, better one," Reade declared. "I'll look over the machinery to make sure that the engine is all right and that I understand the engine and the controls. Her machine-gun is ready for business and we may need it."

Dick stood patiently by, wondering how soon the guard was due to be relieved. If that happened soon, and the knocked-out sentries were discovered, the chance for escape looked like three less than nothing!

"All right," whispered Tom at last. "I can handle her, and there is water enough in the radiator and the gas tanks are filled. Now, then, we must open the doors as noiselessly as possible."

Dick taking the left-hand one, Tom the right, they rolled the doors back. These moved almost noiselessly.

"Here's the way you turn the engine on," Tom whispered, holding the torch and getting Dick up into the cockpit of the craft. "Turn it on as soon as I say, but not a second before."

Placing himself in front of the propeller Tom gave it a few brisk turns.

"Now!" cried Tom, leaping back. The ignition caught at once. Tom clambered over into the cockpit, Prescott now being in the observer's seat forward.

With the wheel in his hands and his feet resting against the controls Tom Reade suddenly dropped all apprehension. He was as much at home now as Prescott was with an automatic pistol in his hand.

Waiting only until the engine had gained its speed without missing, Tom cried:

"Ready, pal!"

Out through the open doorway Reade sent the airplane "taxying" or running along the ground.

Across the field toward them came racing a German aviator with a startled look on his face. He had to jump out of the way as the "taxying" airplane bore down on him. But he reached for his automatic and brought it forth.

"Stop!" he roared. "Turn out the guard!" Bang! bang!

Two bullets whizzed by Tom's head. Prescott fired three shots instantly, one of them taking effect, for the German officer went to earth and lay there, his pistol now silent.

From behind the hangar several members of the guard came rushing from their tents. By the time they were in front of the hangar they could shoot only by guess, and might hit their own comrades in the troop camp. So they fired into the air, wildly, rapidly.

So much shooting was bound to rouse the troop camp, and did. The sentries came out on the jump. While some fired star shells that lighted the sky, others took quick aim with their rifles.

Aiming at the figures on the ground as best he could, just as Reade left the

132

ground for the air, Prescott fired, loaded and fired, jamming in a fresh magazine whenever the automatic became emptied.

Twenty feet up in the air, fifty, a hundred! Tom Reade rose as fast as he could make the machine move. More star shells, and now the anti-aircraft guns came into action.

At three hundred feet above the ground shells exploded about the fugitives. One lucky shot of the enemy would be enough to bring them to earth.

The pistol was now too hot to use further. Dick sat back, closing his eyes, while Reade drove at all the speed he could compel, ever rising higher. Both Americans knew that other anti-aircraft guns further south would be turned upon them.

Finally Tom, after a glance at the barograph, roared at Prescott:

"Five thousand feet up on a dark night, and we're going to fifteen thousand feet. All we now have to fear will be other German aircraft, but there'll be fleets of them sent out to look for us!" Prescott nodded, though he could not hear in the roar of the motors and the rush of the air past him.

A mile below them the blackness of the night was punctured by a lively little volcano of red and yellow jets. A dozen anti-aircraft guns opened fire on the fugitive airplane, whose course must have been telephoned along the line. Some of the shells burst so close that fragments of metal whizzed about the ears of both Americans; some of the shells went far wide of the mark, but at least two of the gunners followed the moving craft for the distance of a mile with an accuracy that caused the two fugitives in the sky the liveliest uneasiness. The gunners were aiming by the sound of the engines.

"Give us fifteen minutes more at this speed,"

Tom roared, "and we'll be back over our own French lines!"

They were soon going at terrific speed, fifteen thousand feet up in the air, when a terrifying peril beset them.

Out of the blackness ahead, bearing straight at them, came a dozen German airplanes in splendid formation!

CHAPTER XXIV

CONCLUSION

"Hurrah!" yelled Tom Reade. "Sink or swim——but never say die! Now we'll give it to 'em, real Yankee Doodle, 'over there' style!"

It sounded like sheer bravado, but Reade was fired with the new genius of the war.

Tom headed straight for the nearest plane, and Dick turned the machine gun loose. Almost immediately he had the great good luck to cripple that enemy and send the craft fluttering down to earth.

But another plane had attempted to go under them with a view to shooting up. It came too near, in the maneuver shot too badly, and Dick let loose with the machine gun again. Down came the enemy plane while Reade took a wide swerve to the right.

So swift and daring had been Reade's tactics that he was through and past the opposing fleet ere the German aviators realized their failure. Now the survivors wheeled and gave chase, though they soon abandoned it, for the plane that Reade drove was a new one and faster than any of his pursuers. For a minute or so more the two Americans survived by sheer good luck. Then they were out of enemy range.

Higher Tom mounted in the air. Dick fairly chattered with the cold, but he kept the machine gun ready for instant use.

A few minutes more, then Tom, shutting off the power for a glide, inquired, at the top of his voice:

"Where do you want to be put down?"

"For choice," Captain Prescott answered, "as close as possible to General Bazain's divisional headquarters."

"I know the place," Tom nodded. "There's an aviation station about three miles beyond there."

Tom threw on the power, straightened away, and three minutes later began to glide again until he was not more than six thousand feet from earth.

"Keep your eyes turned low," Tom counseled. "Soon we ought to see something."

Nor was that "something" long in appearing. Not far ahead, yet so much below them as to look tiny, hundreds of flashes were seen.

"German artillery," Dick told himself.

Another minute, and he beheld flashes turned against the Germans.

"Between the two lines of artillery are the fire trenches of the opposing armies," Prescott realized with a thrill.

Next he found himself, at lower altitude, going squarely over a line of French batteries.

"Now comes the really ticklish work of the night!" Reade shouted back. "When we try for a landing we'll endeavor to make our own crowd understand that, though this is a German machine, it comes on no hostile errand. If we can't make the Frenchmen understand that, then they'll blow us back into the sky as soon as we range low enough!"

Guided by that instinct which is the aviator's best compass at night, Reade steered toward the landing field.

Bang! came the report of a gun below, and a shell exploded dangerously close to the aircraft. Tom switched on an electric light signal beneath the craft to show that a friendly craft sought safe landing. At the same time Dick leaned as far over as he could and waved an arm slowly. Then just ahead a flare began on the ground, next burned up brightly——a can of gasoline lighted and allowed to burn to indicate the neighborhood in which to come down.

Going past and turning, Reade volplaned gracefully earthward, landing just beyond the blazing gasoline.

Instantly they were surrounded by two-score French aviators and mechanicians.

"It is all right!" the cry went up. "They are Americans, though the machine is German."

M. le Commandant Perrault, chief of squadron, stepped rapidly forward, receiving the salute of the two American officers and asking questions at volley-fire speed. His face betrayed amazement, but when the brief narrative had been finished he grasped the hands of each.

"It was splendidly done," he declared.

"And now, sir, on behalf of my friend, may I ask how far we are from the front line?" Tom inquired. "Captain Prescott wishes to return to the trenches immediately."

"It is ten kilometers," replied the commandant. "Yet speed shall not be impossible. Within five minutes I will have here a car that will take Captain

Prescott to the communication trenches, and in that car will be a trench guide."

"And I'm going, too, Dick," Tom added, squeezing his chum's arm. "We have a lot to talk over yet."

As the German airplane had been turned over to Commandant Perrault, Reade had no further concern with that. He bounded into the motor car when it arrived. Later the trench guide conducted them into the front trenches, even to the section from which Prescott had been taken. Major Wells was now, with Captain Holmes and Lieutenant Terry, at a point about a third of a mile to the westward.

Thither Dick and Tom turned their steps, still with the trench guide showing the way. Unexpectedly this little party came upon Major Wells just as the latter was saying:

"The greatest blow to us was the loss of Captain Prescott. Of course he may be a prisoner, and unharmed, but we much fear that he was killed."

"I beg to report, sir," Dick broke in smilingly, as he saluted, "that I was not so indiscreet as to be killed."

Like a flash Major Wells turned upon him. "Prescott!" he cried, "I can't believe it." But he did, just the same, and, coming to his senses, went on hastily:

"General, I have the great happiness of presenting Captain Prescott!"

Again Dick came to the salute, and when it was finished he stood very erect, hands straight at his sides, for he had caught sight, above the horizontal braid on the general's coat, of four stars, instead of the two stars of a major-general. There was but one officer in the United States service who could wear four stars——the American Commander-in-chief.

Under the general's questioning Prescott and Reade, who was also presented, told their stories with soldierly brevity and directness.

"And how do you feel now, Captain?" inquired the Commander-in-chief smiling.

"Utterly happy, sir, for I've realized my sole ambition for months," Captain Dick answered fervently.

"And what was that?"

"To be in France, with General Pershing, and at grips with mankind's enemies."

"You've made a gallant start, Captain," smiled the Commander-in-chief.

"And in that I include your friend, Lieutenant Reade. You are officers after my own heart."

Captain Greg Holmes coming upon this scene, stood back as long as etiquette in the presence of a general demanded, then rushed forward to give joyous greeting to both chums.

Dick and his friends were destined to go even further in the realization of their fondest hopes. Up to this moment the United States was only in the infancy of her part in the great war. Greater days were coming, and did come, and what happened then will be found truthfully set forth in the next volume in this series, which will be published under the title:

"*Uncle Sam's Boys Smash The Germans; Or, Helping the Allies Wind Up the Great World War.*"

THE END

Ingram Content Group UK Ltd.
Milton Keynes UK
UKHW012114250423
420787UK00003B/30